G.I. JOE CLASSIFIED

BY KELLEY SKOVRON

AMULET BOOKS • NEW YORK

Library of Congress Control Number 2022932881

ISBN 978-1-4197-5440-1

Book design by Brenda E. Angelilli

Printed and bound in U.S.A.
10 9 8 7 6 5 4 3 2 1

ABRAMS The Art of Books
195 Broadway, New York, NY 10007
abramsbooks.com

A REAL AMERICAN TOWN

Stan and his mother drove into the town of Springfield late on a Sunday afternoon. He was watching a video on his phone, so he hadn't noticed, but his mother tapped him on the shoulder.

Stan paused his video. "Huh?"

She pointed to a huge LED sign by the side of the road that said:

**WELCOME TO SPRINGFIELD,
A REAL AMERICAN TOWN**

She grinned as they drove past.

"You see, Stanisław?" she asked in her thick Polish accent. "A real American town!"

"Isn't *Chicago* a real American town?" he asked sourly.

She waved her hand dismissively. "Chicago is Chicago."

Stan couldn't argue with that. Chicago was special. Unique. He missed it already. He eyed Springfield's wide streets and orderly buildings suspiciously. Everything was new and streamlined here, with digital billboards and luminous street signs. It was smooth and sleek, like out of some sci-fi movie. He had to admit that it looked neat. But it wasn't Chicago.

"This is a great opportunity for us, Stanisław," his mother said. "DeCobray is one of the most successful companies in the world. My promotion is going to help both of us in many ways."

"I know, Mom." Because this was probably about the twentieth time she'd told him.

"I'll be making more money now, too, so we will be able to afford nice things."

"Can't wait." He would have preferred keeping his friends to having nice things.

"And Springfield has one of the best rated school systems in the country. You will be able to go to any college you want."

"Great." He knew he was supposed to be excited about that, but it seemed so far away. A million years from now.

Her brow furrowed. "That is, if you work hard."

"I will, Mom," Stan said with a hint of irritation. He *always* tried hard in school.

"And no fights!"

Stan winced. "And no fights."

He wasn't a violent boy. He didn't *enjoy* fighting. But when he saw someone get bullied, it made his blood boil. What was he supposed to do—let people get beat up?

Her expression softened. "You miss your friends back in Chicago."

"I miss *everything* back in Chicago, Mom. Just . . . *look* at this place."

Stan gestured to a restaurant they were driving past called Red Rocket, which seemed to have an actual, functional rocket on top. There were no brick townhomes, no winding streets, no deep-dish pizza places. This far from Illinois, they probably hadn't even *heard* of Portillo's.

She frowned. "It is a very *nice* place, Stanisław. DeCobray headquarters is here, and they have invested a lot of money to make it nice for their employees. For *us*."

Stan sighed. "I know, Mom. It's just . . ."

"Not Chicago," she finished.

"Yeah."

They drove through the clean, well-lit, and very un-Chicago town in silence for a little while.

Then his mother said, "Why don't we drive past the school. Maybe when you see it, you will feel more excited."

"Sure, Mom. Whatever you say."

"You can stop the sarcasm, my little Clash."

"Clash" was the nickname his father had given him when he was small because even then he'd been a bit rowdy, and it was the name of his father's favorite rock band. He remembered that when he was really young, he and his father would dance around the apartment, blaring "Rock the Casbah" and "Should I Stay or Should I Go" until his mother yelled at them to turn it down. His father was gone now, but his mother still used that nickname when he was being troublesome or sarcastic. And while she'd never said so, he suspected she liked using it because it reminded her of Stan's father in a tiny way that didn't hurt too much.

A few blocks down, they arrived at Stan's new school. His old middle school back in Chicago hadn't been anything remarkable. Just a big rectangular brick building with a faded sign and an American flag out front. He felt it was what a middle school ought to look like.

Springfield Academy did not look like that. It was a lot bigger, for one thing. He supposed that made sense, since it was a combined middle and high school. But rather than rectangular and brick, it was all swoops and curves, glittering chrome and gleaming windows. If it weren't for the LED sign that said SPRINGFIELD ACADEMY, he might have mistaken it for some kind of fancy tech company.

"See? It is very nice," said his mother as they slowly drove past.

"I guess," he agreed reluctantly.

Then he spotted two students hanging out on the steps in front of the school. They looked to be a couple of years older than Stan. One was a boy with longish hair who wore a dark camo jacket. He sat on the steps slumped forward staring down at his phone. He looked relaxed, but there was also an intense gleam in his eye that that drew Stan right in, though he couldn't say why. The other student was a girl with long black hair and glasses. She wore a black leather jacket and leaned against the hand-rail. The girl appeared to be talking to someone, though it didn't seem like it was the boy. She might have had ear-buds in, but Stan couldn't see because of her hair. There was a slight smile on her face, like everything was a tiny bit amusing to her but not enough to actually get excited about.

"Who are *they*?" he wondered aloud.

"*Tch.*" His mother made a disapproving noise. "Hooligans is what they are. Loitering in front of the school like that."

"*Hooligans*, Mom?"

"Look at them!" She gestured to the pair as they drove past. "I tell you, those two are no good!"

Of course, that just made Stan want to know them even more.

CHAPTER 2

A REAL TECH TOWN

DeCobray had hired a moving company to transport everything from their old apartment in Chicago to their nice new house, so it was already stacked up in neat boxes on the bare living room floor when they arrived.

Their Chicago apartment had been tiny, so it didn't take Stan and his mother long to unpack. And since the new house was so much bigger, it still felt empty when they were done.

Stan's mother rubbed her hands together gleefully. "We will just have to go furniture shopping next weekend!"

"Yay." Stan was not a fan of shopping.

That night, he had a hard time falling asleep in the unfamiliar house, but eventually he drifted off. When he woke the following morning, his mother had already left for the office. That was nothing new. His mother had more or less *lived* at the DeCobray regional office in Chicago, and he hadn't expected that to change now that she was working at the world headquarters.

Stan got dressed in jeans and a black T-shirt, then made a few half-hearted swipes at his shaggy brown hair. He ate a bowl of cereal, then grabbed his backpack and used his phone to navigate the walk to his new school.

Springfield Academy looked just as strange and unschool-like as it had the night before, although now beneath the school name, the LED sign also said:

> IT'S TIME TO MAXIMIZE
> YOUR POTENTIAL!

"Maximize my potential?" he muttered to himself as he started climbing the steps to the school entrance.

"That is correct," came a female voice with a Slavic accent nearly as thick as his mother's, although he couldn't place the country.

It was the girl with glasses from the night before. She stood by the front doors of the school at the top of the steps, looking at him expectantly.

"You are Stanisław Migda of Kraków, Poland, correct?"

Stan was born in Poland, but his father had been American, so he had dual citizenship. And since he'd grown up mostly in Chicago, he didn't have an accent. Well, not a *Polish* accent, anyway. He might have a little bit of a Chicago one.

"Yeah, that's me," he said as he approached.

"Excellent. I am Baroness Anastasia Cisarovna. You may call me Baroness."

"Oh, uh . . . Nice to meet you . . . Baroness." He'd expected her to say that he could call her Anastasia. Or maybe even Annie. It felt weirdly formal to call her by a title, but he'd never met a baroness before, so maybe this was normal.

She smiled. "Such a polite boy. I like you already."

"Thanks?" He felt himself blush.

"DeCobray wants its international students to feel at home," she said in a crisp, businesslike tone. "Which is why I, as a fellow European, have been assigned to be your peer orientation counselor. It is my responsibility to help you adjust to the exceptional student life at Springfield Academy. First, you will need this."

She handed him a pair of earbuds that hooked over his ears. They were connected with a thin strip of soft material.

"What is it?" he asked.

"Put it on," she commanded.

He obediently fixed the buds to his ears, the material stretched snugly across the base of his skull. It was surprisingly comfortable, and the back part was completely hidden by his hair.

"State your full name and grade," she told him.

"Stanisław Migda, eighth grade."

Anastasia's eyes seemed to look at something directly in front of her, but there was nothing there. Then she nodded in satisfaction and waved her hand. "Voice print accepted."

"What does that mean?" he asked.

"Say 'Activate display.'"

"OK, uh, activate display?"

A hologram display screen suddenly appeared in the air in front of him, kind of like a video game interface. Text at the top flashed, "Good morning, Stanisław," for a moment, then disappeared. In one corner he could see the time and current temperature. When he looked at Anastasia, a small text bubble appeared beside her that stated her full name and grade ten. He turned to look at other students entering the building and could see their names, grades, and even their hometowns.

"Whoa."

"Yes, whoa." Anastasia seemed pleased with his reaction. "The Lyre XR device is the very latest in DeCobray technology. These headsets can be found nowhere else in the world."

"But we get them?" he asked.

"Students at Springfield Academy are fortunate

enough to be a beta test group for this revolutionary new technology," said Anastasia. "Follow me."

The display was pretty minimal, but walking while it hovered in his peripheral vision still took some getting used to.

"Can other people see what I'm seeing?" he asked.

"No, it is not a hologram. The Lyre device interacts directly with your neural receptors to create the images inside your head."

"It's connected to my brain?" That sounded creepy and he reached up to take it off.

"Of course not—that would be a terrible invasion of privacy," Anastasia said quickly. "The Lyre is a one-way, noninvasive projection utilizing brain wave entrainment and cranial electrical stimulation."

"Oh, uh, sure." He had no idea what any of that meant. But as long as it wasn't connecting to his brain, he supposed it was fine.

They walked through the hallways of Springfield Academy together. Anastasia was telling him something about the history of the school, but he kept getting distracted by the names and grades that popped up next to the face of every person he saw.

He did notice that the other students gave them a wide berth, and some even looked down at the ground as they passed. Maybe because she was a baroness? Should *he* be doing that? He wasn't sure . . .

Then he noticed the classrooms.

"Are all the walls in here glass?" he asked as he peered into one room. It had rows of sleek white desks and surprisingly comfy-looking chairs, but it was otherwise empty. "Doesn't that get distracting, seeing people walk by while you're trying to focus on the teacher."

"No, no," she said dismissively. "It's one-way glass. On the inside it looks like mirrors."

Stan stared at her. "That's a little weird."

"It is necessary for the school administrators to make certain that the education received by students at Springfield Academy is perfect in every way."

"I . . . guess that makes sense." It didn't actually make sense to him, but Anastasia seemed really sure of herself, and he didn't want to contradict her.

"You will notice there are no projectors or electronic whiteboards in any of the classrooms," she said.

"Huh, that's true."

"That is because all your educational materials are displayed on your Lyre device."

He tapped the bud on his ear. "So all my textbooks are in here, too?"

"Textbooks, as well as any multimedia the teacher utilizes during the class period. There is no need for projectors and whiteboards, and you can customize the display to best suit your learning style."

"This is incredible," said Stan. "I can't believe I've never heard about this before."

"That is because we cannot talk about it outside Springfield, or post anything about it on social media until DeCobray is ready for a public launch. In fact, I'm afraid I must ask that you hand over your personal phone for the time being."

She held out her hand.

He stared at it. "You want me to give you my phone?"

"Your mother has already signed the consent form." There was a hint of impatience in her voice.

"But . . . What if I have to text her or something?"

"She is a DeCobray employee, correct?" Now her voice bordered on irritation.

"Uh, yeah?"

"Her contact information and yours are all in the DeCobray database. You can use your Lyre device to call or message her at any time, just like you would on a phone."

"Well, I guess if my mom is cool with it . . ."

It wasn't the first time she had forgotten to tell him about something like this. That was the trouble with having a brilliant engineer for a parent. Sometimes the little stuff escaped her.

He handed Anastasia his phone. "So, is there anything this Lyre device *can't* do?"

She smiled. Once again, she seemed pleased when he showed how impressed he was with the device. "Well, at this time, it runs only DeCobray software. No third-party apps."

He grinned. "So no games?"

Her black eyebrow raised over her glasses. "Oh, I wouldn't say that exactly. But for now you must get to your first class. My friend Michel and I usually hang out at the Red Rocket after school. Meet us there and we will show you some of the Lyre's more amusing tricks."

"R-Really?" An older student was willing to take this much time with him? And a baroness, no less?

"Of course," she said, back to her brisk, no-nonsense tone. "I'm always thrilled to have another European at our school. Don't worry, little Stanisław, I will take you under my wing."

He felt himself blushing again. "Thanks."

Anastasia dropped him off at his first class and said goodbye. He felt a little embarrassed at the special treatment, but only one person in the class seemed to even notice. A tall Black boy named Julien March, grade eight, from Kansas City, according to Stan's Lyre display.

Their eyes made contact and Julien nodded, his expression unreadable. Then he turned back to face the front of the class.

Stan found the only empty seat in the room and sat down. A moment later, a face appeared directly in front of him and he involuntarily flinched. It was so high-def that for a moment he thought the man was actually standing there. But he quickly realized it was a projection from his Lyre device.

The man had thick iron-gray hair neatly combed back and sharp, elegant features. He wore a trim burgundy suit with a yellow tie and pocket square.

"Good morning, students of Springfield Academy," he said in a rich, soothing baritone.

"Good morning, Principal Zartan," the other students in Stan's class said.

Apparently everyone was seeing the same thing on their Lyre devices. This must be how they did morning announcements. At Stan's old school, it had been over a crackling PA speaker.

"Another fine day of learning is before us," Principal Zartan said. "Be sure to study hard. I look forward to seeing all your metrics at the end of the day."

Metrics? Maybe with these Lyre devices, all their classwork was automatically tracked and graded. Stan supposed that made sense, but it also added a layer of pressure to everything.

"One item of note," continued the principal. "Please

welcome our midyear transfer student, eighth grader Stanisław Migda, and congratulate his mother, Leokadia Migda, on her promotion to DeCobray corporate headquarters."

Then a picture of Stan and his mother appeared on the display. It was a picture Stan had never seen before. Just the two of them standing there, smiling goofy smiles. On the whole not terrible, but still. The entire school had just seen it, and now everyone would know him as the transfer kid.

He sank lower in his seat. Fortunately, everyone seemed to be ignoring him. Except Julien, who gave him a wry smile.

Then a message appeared on Stan's display.

JULIEN: Welcome to Springfield!

A REAL UNEASY TOWN

The Lyre device might not be able to run actual video games, but it almost made school *feel* like a game. Every class featured interactive elements, where Stan and the other students were moving things around on a virtual display only they could see. His Lyre could track his hand movements with perfect precision, and if he needed to type something, his Lyre could turn any flat surface into a virtual keyboard. It probably would have looked bizarre for anyone who didn't have a Lyre device to see a bunch of eighth graders waving their hands around in the air or tapping their bare desks. But since everyone was wearing one, it didn't matter.

The mirrored classroom walls felt creepy at first. All four interior walls of every room reflected off each other, so it looked like an endless army of identical students that stretched out in all directions into infinity. But since the teacher could share media with their Lyre devices, they would make the walls appear to change their setting. One teacher made it feel like they were sitting in the middle of the forest. Another made it look like a beach. And the classroom not only looked like a new location but sounded like it as well. Audio effects like the gentle rustle of trees in the wind or the quiet rush of the waves made it really feel like they had been somehow transported. And it was always somewhere peaceful and quiet, so the setting actually made it easier for Stan to concentrate.

The classwork was genuinely challenging, but the interactivity made it almost feel easy. Stan never had to force himself to pay attention to his teachers, which probably helped a lot. And he was happy to discover that teachers didn't assign homework at Springfield Academy, because they were supposed to "support well-rounded students who are expected to participate in after-school clubs, athletics, and community activities." Stan had never been interested in sports, so he didn't know what sort of after-school thing he might join. He wondered if Anastasia might have some suggestions.

Finding his way to the Red Rocket after school was easy thanks to the map and directions displayed on his Lyre device. But as he approached the sleek, white restaurant with its realistic rocket on top, he started to get a little nervous. Was it really OK for him to hang out with tenth graders? Maybe she'd been trolling him? But Stan knew kids who liked to prank back in Chicago, and Anastasia didn't seem like the type.

Besides, if she had sincerely invited him, and he didn't show up, that would be super rude.

So he took a deep breath and pushed open the door.

Along the left side of the restaurant interior was a long counter, and on the right side was a line of booths, with a row of small tables down the middle. It looked kind of like a diner, except everything was somehow not stained or covered in a greasy film. It didn't really have that fried food smell either, so Stan suspected it was one of those health food "diners."

Well, no place was perfect.

He spotted Anastasia at a large corner booth in the back of the restaurant. She was sitting with the boy in dark camo he'd seen the previous evening. Stan's Lyre display now informed him it was Michel LeClerc, Grade 10, from New Orleans.

Michel looked just as intense as he had the night before, and Stan hesitated a moment. But then Anastasia spotted him and waved him over.

"Here is our new pet eighth grader," Anastasia told Michel as Stan approached.

Michel's eyes narrowed as he looked at Stan, like he was sizing him up.

"This one? You sure?"

"Oh yes," said Anastasia. "I looked over his records. He's perfect."

"My records?" asked Stan, trying to hide his nervousness as he sat down at the booth.

"School records and such," said Anastasia. "As your

designated peer counselor, I was given access to whatever was deemed necessary to ease your transition."

"Oh . . ."

Stan wondered how much she knew about him. Private stuff? What was it about his records that made him "perfect," and for what? He wanted to ask all those questions, but Anastasia had an aloof presence that made it difficult for him to relax, and Michel was downright intimidating.

"We should put that to the test," said Michel.

"In a moment," said Anastasia. "Stanisław, how was your first day at Springfield Academy?"

"It was pretty amazing," said Stan. "I don't think I've ever had a school day go by so fast. These Lyre devices are incredible. Once people outside Springfield start using them, it's going to change the world."

Michel snorted. "For those who can afford them, anyway."

"Oh, right, I guess they're going to be pretty expensive," said Stan. "But maybe DeCobray will donate some to schools? It would really make a difference at places like my old public school in Chicago."

"Yes, Michel," Anastasia said with a strange smirk. "Think of the children."

He shrugged. "I suppose getting them hooked early would be an investment down the line."

"You'll have to forgive Michel," Anastasia told Stan. "He has a mercenary mind."

"But I always get the job done," said Michel.

"Do you have a part-time job?" Stan asked him.

Michel seemed to find that amusing. "Something like that. Speaking of which, let's get out of here."

"Good idea," said Anastasia. "I promised I'd show Stanisław a few of the more amusing tricks Lyre devices can do."

Michel rolled his eyes as he slid out of the booth. "Don't baby him too much."

"Not where it counts," she promised.

As Stan got up from the booth to follow Anastasia and Michel, he still felt uneasy. These tenth graders had so many inside jokes, he wasn't sure he knew what they were talking about half the time. Then he glanced at the empty dishes on the table.

"Don't you guys need to pay your bill?"

They both laughed at that, and Anastasia even patted him on the head in a patronizing kind of way. Then they continued down the aisle toward the doors.

Stan followed behind them, his unease growing. Judging by their response, he had the feeling they were walking out on the bill. Yet none of the servers said anything. So maybe they had a tab? Or maybe the kids of DeCobray employees had some sort of deal with the restaurant? But it didn't feel like that for some reason, and it made him uncomfortable. Walking out on a bill wasn't just breaking a dumb rule. It meant someone working here wasn't getting paid.

But what could he do about it?

He paused at the door and glanced back into the restaurant. Still, nobody looked at them. In fact, it was almost like people were *purposefully* not looking. Like they were all afraid?

Except for one booth. A boy with a black hoodie that was pulled low over his face sat with a red-headed girl in a yellow tank top.

Stan felt a jolt when the girl looked directly at him with her piercing blue eyes. Then she slowly raised her eyebrow.

It felt like she was challenging him. Like she was asking:

Well? What can *you do about it?*

A REAL MEAN TOWN

Stan followed Anastasia and Michel through the clean, well-lit downtown Springfield as night began to fall. He still felt uncomfortable. Maybe even a little ashamed. His older cousins back in Chicago waited tables, and he knew how hard they worked and how much every tip meant to them. Even worse, in some restaurants, if a customer walked out on a bill, it was the server who had to cover the loss.

He wasn't so sure about these kids anymore. But

what *could* he do? Make up some excuse that he had to go and . . . then what? Sit in an unfamiliar empty house and wait for his mother to get home? That sounded pretty depressing. Plus, if he bailed now, he could forget about any more help from Anastasia.

And maybe he was jumping to conclusions. Perhaps they'd already paid the bill before he got there, and the laugh had been more like: *Duh, we already paid, little eighth grader.* Yeah, that was probably it.

"OK, let's see . . ." Michel swiped his hand in front of his face, like he was interacting with his Lyre device. "He's this way."

Michel abruptly turned a corner, with Anastasia and Stan following.

"He?" Stan asked Anastasia.

"We're meeting a . . . *friend*," said Anastasia.

Michel chuckled at that but continued forward.

"You can share your GPS location with other people on your Lyre?" asked Stan.

"Something like that," said Anastasia. "You know, Stanisław, the Lyre does many useful things, but you can also have a lot of fun with it. Have you tried out the filters yet?"

"No, I saw there was a filter function, but I figured it was just to change the colors and stuff like social media apps."

"Oh, it's much more than that, Stanisław," said Anastasia. "Why don't you give it a try."

He tapped the small filter icon in the lower corner of his display, and he was presented with several options: Toon Town, Gotham, Van Gogh, and Cyberspace. On impulse, he selected the last one.

The world around him flickered, then transformed. It was still the same place, but now normal streets looked like metal lit up with glowing streaks of light that shifted color over time. It was as if he was suddenly in some sort of city of the future with gleaming spires and hologram advertisements.

"Amazing," he whispered.

"Isn't it?"

He turned to Anastasia, and even she looked different. Her features sharper, her eyes brighter. Instead of a regular leather jacket, she was wearing some sort of black *Matrix*-looking outfit.

"Incredible!"

"Try another one," she suggested.

He switched to Toon Town, and like the name suggested, he was suddenly living in a cheery cartoon world, with curved buildings and dancing streetlamps. Anastasia looked like a cartoonist had drawn her, exaggerating her intense eyebrows, her long black hair, and the smirk on her lips. Even the moon, which was just beginning to rise, had a smiling face on it now.

He switched to Gotham, and as he expected, the whole town changed to a dark and brooding metropolis, like something out of a Batman movie. Everything was dimly lit and moody. It even looked like it was raining, despite the fact that it wasn't.

He switched the filter off and shook his head. "Wow, that's intense."

"It does take some getting used to," she agreed. "But over time you'll adjust. And this is only the beginning. DeCobray will continue to make new filters for us to test out, and eventually we'll even be able to create custom filters. Imagine, making the world look exactly like you've always wished it did."

Stan's mind reeled at the idea. To think something like this would eventually be released into the wide world. It would be like the smartphone revolution. Maybe even bigger.

Michel abruptly stopped. "Here he comes."

Then he looked expectantly down a nearby alley.

Stan peered down the dark, narrow passage and saw Julien walking toward them. He didn't notice Stan and the others yet and instead frowned thoughtfully, seemingly focused on his Lyre display. Every few seconds, he made a few quick gestures, like he was typing in midair.

"Well, if it isn't Julien March," Michel called to him.

Julien froze. He swiped his hand, like he was clearing whatever was on his display, and looked uneasily at Michel.

"Oh, uh, hey, man . . ."

Michel sauntered down the alley toward the boy. He was smiling, but there was something about it that didn't seem friendly at all.

"Julien, it seems your metrics have been a little irregular lately."

Julien looked even more unsettled. "I-Irregular?"

Michel stood directly in front of him now. He was several inches shorter than Julien, but somehow he was far more intimidating.

"You didn't happen to tinker with your Lyre device, did you?"

"Me? Tinker?" Julien looked extremely guilty. Clearly he was not good at lying. "W-Well, you know what they say, hacker's gotta hack. I was just looking under the hood a little, you know? Just curious."

"Yes, I can sympathize with your curiosity," Michel said coolly. "The trouble is, tampering with your Lyre device in *any way* is strictly prohibited. And this is not your first offense. You were warned what would happen if you did it again."

"Right . . ." Julien's eyes darted around like he was looking for an escape. He seemed genuinely frightened now.

"What's going on?" Stan demanded.

"Michel is on the . . . disciplinary committee," Anastasia said.

"Wait, that was the job he was talking about? We

weren't meeting a friend, we were hunting down Julien for *punishment*?"

Julien had begun to edge away while they talked, but Michel put his arm around his shoulders, like they were buddies. Except they clearly weren't.

"You're lucky it's me who found you." Michel looked up at Julien with his unfriendly smile. "I've always liked you, Julien. I respect your computer skills. Your rebelliousness. That's why I told them I would handle it. Because you know, if *they* got to you, well . . ." Michel shrugged. "Nice knowing you."

"I get it, I get it," said Julien. "I swear I won't do it again."

Michel sighed like a disappointed parent. "That's what you said *last* time, buddy. So for my own peace of mind, I'm going to give you something to help you remember."

Then he punched Julien in the stomach. The taller boy crumpled up and started heaving. With a look of disgust, Michel shoved him to the ground, where he lay gasping for breath.

"Hey! Get away from him!" Stan's anger flared. He couldn't stand seeing someone get bullied. It was like a trigger for him. He could already feel his face heating up as he strode toward Michel, his fist clenched.

Michel gave Stan an irritated look, then turned to Anastasia. "I thought you said he was *perfect*."

She shrugged. "It seemed like he was. His student discipline record is *filled* with incidents of violence."

"I'm not violent," seethed Stan through his teeth. "I just have an impulse control problem, and I *hate* bullies!"

"Oh, I see." Michel did not look even a little intimidated. "So it would upset you if I did . . . this?"

He spun on his heel and kicked the prone Julien in the face.

And Stan's mind went red.

Back in Chicago, Stan had a reputation for being bad-tempered, ever since his father died. He never started a fight, but he was always ready to finish one. OK, sometimes he might have even gone looking for one to finish now and then. He just got so *frustrated*. It wasn't *fair* that the strong constantly picked on the weak and everyone else let it happen. But not Stan. He would *make* things fair.

That's why his fist crashed into Michel's face.

Michel staggered back, rubbing his cheek. But then he smiled. "Not bad, kid. It's a real shame you didn't work out."

Then in a blink, he popped Stan right in the eye.

Stan stumbled as the pain lanced through his face. He could almost feel his brain bounce around in his skull. A concussion was likely imminent, so he'd have to finish this quick. But when he went for Michel again, the older boy easily evaded him, then stepped in and punished him with a blow to the ribs. They traded a few more punches and even with the onset of a mild concussion, it dawned on Stan that Michel wasn't some overconfident bully. This kid had *combat training* and Stan was in big trouble.

"It really is a shame," he heard Anastasia's voice behind him.

He half turned, not sure what to expect and unwilling to take his eyes off Michel completely. So he wasn't at all prepared when she kicked him square in the chest.

The wind whooshed out of him, and he nearly joined Julien on the ground. But no. He wouldn't go down. He *couldn't* go down. His father had gone down and never

gotten back up. That wouldn't be him. Not today. Not *ever*.
So he straddled the fallen Julien and stood his ground.

"He's a sturdy one, isn't he?" said Michel as they circled him and Julien.

"He's got the grit," agreed Anastasia. "But apparently he has some sort of hero complex."

"Ooo." Michel gave him a mock regretful look. "That just won't do in Springfield."

Stan forced himself to straighten despite the pain and lifted his fists. "Fine, I'll take you both on at once."

"No need."

Suddenly, the red-headed girl and the boy in the black hoodie were beside him. He didn't know where they came from, but they looked ready to fight.

Michel took one look at the boy in the hoodie, and his lip curled into a snarl. "You!"

Then he lunged.

What happened next was like one single swift but unhurried motion. Michel came at the boy with a roundhouse punch. The boy blocked it and at the same time shoved his palm into Michel's chin. Michel's head started to snap back, but the boy grabbed the nape of his neck, pulled him forward, kneed him in the stomach, then swept his legs out from under him so he fell to the ground beside Julien. Then the boy dropped to one knee and delivered a single punch to Michel's chest. The smooth grace of the sequence was almost beautiful. Like a dance.

They all stared down at the wheezing, gasping, semiconscious Michel for a moment.

Then the red-headed girl looked at Anastasia. "You want a turn?"

Anastasia sniffed. "Please, you are not worth the effort. Come on, Michel. Let us go."

She grabbed Michel's arm and hauled him to his feet.

"I thought you showed real promise, Stanisław," Anastasia said over her shoulder as she helped Michel stagger back up the alley. "But I guess you are a fool like all the rest."

Then they were gone.

CHAPTER 5

>>>>>>>>>>> A REAL KIND TOWN >>>>>>>>>>>

"You OK, Julien?" The red-haired girl grasped his hand and helped him to his feet. She wasn't big, but the muscles that surged beneath her yellow tank top made it clear that she was plenty strong. "Let's get you patched up."

"Thanks, Scarlett," he said through his swollen, bloody face. "You too, Zoro-me."

The boy in the hoodie nodded. Now that Stan was able to get a better look at him, he could see that scars crisscrossed the boy's face. They looked old but deep.

"Hey, new kid," said Scarlett. "You OK?"

"Yeah, sure," said Stan, because he wasn't about to admit that he hurt in at least three different places, including his lower lip, which was split, and an eye that was probably going to swell shut pretty soon.

"Uh-huh." She squinted like she didn't believe him, which was fair. "Why don't you come along anyway."

Stan had already made one bad decision tonight blindly following kids he didn't know. He didn't plan on making that mistake again. These two weren't even showing up on his Lyre device.

"Where do you want me to go?" he asked. "And also *who are you?*"

"I guess I can't blame you for being a little wary after what just happened. My name is Shana, but people call me Scarlett." She nodded to the boy in the hoodie. "That's Ichi No Zoro-me. People just call him Zoro-me."

The boy's name sounded Japanese, and he bowed in the Japanese style when Scarlett introduced him, but he looked white and had short blond hair. His scarred face had a thoughtful, somewhat solemn expression, as though he was always carefully considering everything around him. He'd even looked like that as he was kicking Michel's butt.

"Zoro-me and I are both tenth graders at Springfield Academy," said Scarlett. "What about you?"

He noticed that neither Scarlett nor Zoro-me were wearing Lyre devices. That was probably why their IDs hadn't shown up. "Stan. Eighth grade. You go to Springfield but you don't have Lyres?"

"We *have* them," said Scarlett. "We only wear them when it's absolutely necessary."

"Why?"

"So people like Michel can't follow us around."

"Oh yeah . . ." He turned to Julien. "I'm assuming you didn't actually share your GPS with him."

Julien tried to smile but winced and touched his bruised face. "You kidding? That is the last thing I want. In fact, I'm pretty sure one of the things I got in trouble for was trying to mask my location."

"*One* of the things?" asked Stan.

"Hacker's gotta hack," he said, like it was an actual explanation.

"We can talk more about that later," said Scarlett. "Right now, let's get you fixed up at the dojo."

"What do you mean *dojo*?" said Stan. "Like a martial arts school?"

"You'll see. But first." She pulled out a shiny metallic-looking bag with a zip seal and held it open. "Lyres. In here."

"Oooh, nice!" said Julien, and quickly dropped his into the bag.

They looked expectantly at Stan.

"What does the bag do?" he asked cautiously.

"Static shielding," said Scarlett. "It just keeps it from contacting the DeCobray servers."

He was still reluctant to trust, but these people had just saved his butt, and he had to agree that not being tracked by Michel was a good thing. So after a moment, he nodded and dropped his into the bag.

"Great!" Scarlett sealed up the bag, then began walking down the alley. "Follow me."

Stan sighed. "Sure, why not. It isn't like this night could get any crazier."

Scarlett looked over her shoulder at him. "Never say that in Springfield."

"Yeah, I'm starting to wonder if there's more to this place than just fancy street signs."

"You have no idea."

Stan and Julien fell in behind Scarlett, with Zoro-me bringing up the rear.

"Hey man," Julien said to Stan. "Thanks for sticking up for me. I mean, you don't even *know* me."

"Honestly, I had no idea what I was getting into. I saw Michel picking on you and it set me off. But really Zoro-me was the one who actually did something." Stan turned back to Zoro-me. "What was that back there? Some kind of martial art?"

Zoro-me nodded.

"You don't say much, huh?"

"No," he said.

"Ah." Stan wasn't quite sure how to respond to that. It didn't seem like the other boy was trying to be rude or anything. He'd just answered the question honestly and directly, without any elaboration.

A short time later, they reached a building with a sign that said ARASHIKAGE DOJO. From the outside, it looked like every other building in Springfield. Sleek, modern. But once they went inside, it felt as though they had been transported to the sort of serene, bare space that Stan had only ever seen in old samurai movies, with rice-paper sliding doors and a large open space covered with a tatami mat.

"Everyone needs to take off their shoes at the door," said Scarlett. Then she turned to Zoro-me. "You want to get your uncle?"

He nodded, then headed through a doorway in the back while the rest of them took off their shoes.

Scarlett took some round cushions from a cabinet and tossed them on the mat for them to sit on.

"So . . ." Stan plopped down on a cushion. "Zoro-me's uncle owns this dojo?"

Scarlett sat down on hers with a lot more grace. "He actually has two uncles and they co-own it."

"Guh . . ." said Julien as he gingerly sat on his cushion.

"I guess that's why Zoro-me is so good at martial arts," said Stan.

"Yeah, he's . . ." Scarlett trailed off and her brow furrowed.

Stan was about to ask her what was wrong, but then he felt it. He couldn't say exactly how, but there was suddenly a *presence* in the room. A dark, *deadly* aura that made his pulse race and his palms sweat.

"W-W-Wha . . ." he stuttered.

But Scarlett just rolled her eyes. "Konichiwa, Hādo-sensei."

A deep voice seemed to come from everywhere and nowhere at once.

"Okaerinasai, Shana-chan."

Then, as if by magic, a thin old Japanese man dressed in black robes appeared before them. He looked like he could have been eighty or even older, but he did not seem frail in any way. In fact, Stan didn't know if he'd ever seen a scarier person in his life.

Scarlett didn't seem impressed, but there was a hint of a smile, as if she was fond of him but didn't want to show it.

"Stan, this is Uncle Hādo. Uncle Hādo, this is the latest dumb American teenager to cause trouble in Springfield."

"I see . . ." Hādo scrutinized Stan in a way that did not put him any more at ease. "I give him a week. Maybe two."

"To what?" asked Stan.

Hādo smiled coldly. "Continue breathing."

"Hādo, are you frightening the guests?"

Another old Japanese man dressed in a bright orange robe entered from the back room, followed by Zoro-me. Stan guessed that this was Zoro-me's other uncle. But he seemed like the exact opposite of Hādo. He was round and cheerful and exuded the kind of warmth that you might find coming from a kindergarten teacher.

This time, Scarlett did break into a smile. "Konichiwa, Yawarakai-sensei."

"Konichiwa, Shana-chan," he said in a voice like warm honey.

"Shana-chan is no guest," said Hādo. "She practically lives here."

"True," said Yawarakai. "But what of these poor injured boys?"

"You are too indulgent." Hādo's steely gaze once more fell on Stan. "Fear can be a wonderful instructor, and it could be exactly what they need."

"Hai, hai," Yawarakai said placatingly as he knelt beside Julien and began examining his injuries. "As usual, I'm sure the truth lies somewhere between our two viewpoints." He opened a leather case. "We'll have you boys fixed up soon. I promise."

"Not *too* soon, I hope," said Hādo. "Pain is also a wonderful instructor."

Stan watched with fascination as Yawarakai began to grind up dried herbs with a mortar and pestle. It really was like something out of an old samurai movie.

"Found some new club members, *Scarlett*?"

A new voice came from right behind Stan, and it was so unexpected that he flinched. *How did all these people keep appearing out of nowhere?*

This time it was another boy, maybe eleventh grade. He looked to be of Japanese descent and was dressed in a white hoodie and jeans. He was almost the mirror opposite of Zoro-me. Not just because of his dark hair and white clothes, but because where Zoro-me was silent and reserved, this boy exuded a kind of confidence—a swagger almost. And he seemed to enjoy the sound of his own voice.

"Seriously, Shana-chan," he said to her in a teasing tone. "Are you assembling an *army*?"

She shrugged. "Maybe I am."

"Okaerinasai, Tomisaburo-kun," Yawarakai said pleasantly as he began to apply a poultice to Julien's cheek.

"Yeah, yeah, tadaima, Ojisan," said Tomisaburo as he walked over to a mini fridge set against one wall and took out an energy drink. "And I told you, I want everyone to call me Tommy from now on. That includes you."

"*I* have no intention of calling you anything other than the name your father gave you," said Hādo.

Tommy ignored that and turned his attention to Julien and Stan. "So what do we have here?"

"Eighth graders who got caught up in Michel's strong-arm tactics," said Scarlett.

"Huh." Tommy took a long chug of his drink. "I hope you gave as good as you got."

"Stan did," said Julien. "The only fighting I'm good at is in a Smash Bros tournament."

Tommy looked at Stan with more interest. "Oh yeah? You were OK at least?"

"He's got a lot of potential," said Scarlett. "Even your brother thinks so."

Zoro-me nodded.

Stan didn't exactly like being talked about as if he wasn't there, but he didn't mind the compliments. And Tommy looked impressed by Zoro-me's assessment, which made Stan wonder something.

"So, Tommy . . ." He wasn't sure how to ask the question without sounding rude. "You and Zoro-me . . . are brothers?"

Tommy grinned. "What, don't we look alike?"

"Uh . . ."

Tommy laughed. "Just joking—Stan, is it? Listen, man, you've got to lighten up a little."

"Or *you* need to be more serious," said Hādo.

Tommy bowed mockingly to the old man. "*Hai!* Thank you for the instruction, Hādo-sensei!"

Hādo sighed as though it genuinely caused him pain. "American teenagers . . ."

"Stan, your question is understandable," Yawarakai said as he applied a paste to Julien's lip. "As it happens, Tomisa—" He stopped himself. "*Tommy*-kun is our nephew by blood. We took in Ichi No Zoro-me-kun when he was a little boy after he survived a terrible car accident that killed the rest of his family."

The car accident explained the scars on Zoro-me's face. But even worse was the loss of his entire family. Stan's own father had died, so he had some idea what it felt like. He couldn't imagine losing his mother, too.

"I'm so sorry, Zoro-me," he said, knowing it wasn't enough but also knowing there was nothing he could say that would be.

Yawarakai moved over to kneel in front of Stan and began applying a poultice to his swelling eye.

"To make matters worse," continued Yawarakai, "Ichi No Zoro-me-kun hardly remembers anything of his life before the accident."

Stan at least had some cherished memories of his own father. The idea of losing even those . . .

"He couldn't even remember his own name," said

Hādo. "That is why I decided we should call him Ichi No Zoro-me. It means . . . eh . . . *Snake-eyes*, you know? The worst roll of the dice. Because of his terrible luck."

Hādo laughed like this was some great joke, but Stan didn't find it funny, and clearly neither did Tommy or Scarlett. Even Yawarakai's smile looked pained.

But Zoro-me walked over to Hādo, squeezed his shoulder, and nodded.

"Well, at least *you* get it," said Hādo. "My favored pupil."

"Whatever, teacher's pet," said Tommy.

"*Anyway*," said Scarlett. "Tommy actually had a good idea a minute ago. Stan? Julien? Zoro-me and I recently started an after-school club. You should both join."

Stan tried to ask what kind of club, but Yawarakai was smearing his split lip with a tingling ointment, so it came out more like "Wa kan ah cla?"

Tommy smirked. "The *Average Joes*. Dorkiest club name ever, right?"

"Nobody asked you, Tommy," said Scarlett. Then she turned back to Julien and Stan. "We want to help out other students who get hassled by jerks like Michel. Well? What do you say?"

Stan eyed Tommy's mocking grin. "Oh, uh . . ."

But then Tommy's expression grew serious. "Actually you should do it. Unless you want to be just another lab rat."

"Lab rat?" asked Stan. "What are you talking about?"

Tommy finished off his drink, tossed the can across the room into the recycling bin, then started walking toward the back rooms.

"Just join the dorky club, kid," he said on his way out.

A REAL FANTASY TOWN

Yawarakai insisted that they all stay for dinner, so they knelt around a large table and had something called nikujaga, which was like a meat and potato stew but sweeter. Stan didn't have much experience using chopsticks, but at least he was better than Julien.

It was around nine P.M. by the time he left the dojo. He was worried that his mother would be mad about him being out so late, but the house was dark when he arrived. In fact, she didn't get home until around ten, and she looked completely exhausted.

"You OK, Mom?" he asked as she poured herself a drink, then flopped down on their tiny couch.

She smiled wearily. "Sorry, I'm a little tired. How was your first day of school? I hope my little Clash did not cause any trouble."

If he told her about Michel and Anastasia, he'd have to admit that he got into a fight on the first day, which would make her mad. So instead, he said, "It was, uh, fine. We all get these cool devices."

He hadn't put them back in his ears after he left the dojo, so he fished them out of his pocket and held them up.

"Oh, yes, the Lyre devices. We use them at work, too." She pushed her hair back to show him an identical device in her ear. "They are so handy, I already wonder how I got anything done without one."

"I didn't realize you were part of the beta test program, too," he said.

"The whole town is," she said. "Even people who do not work for DeCobray or go to Springfield Academy are eligible to receive one. Very exciting, isn't it?"

"Yeah . . ."

It *had* been exciting when he first got his. After all, it did some really cool stuff. But now he wasn't so sure. Could Michel track any kid in school? Maybe anyone in town? And why did he *have* that capability? Stan sure didn't. Who else could track people? And what else could they find out besides location? Messages? Phone calls? He'd heard of smartphones being hacked so they could be turned into microphones, spying on their owners. Was someone listening to his conversation with his mother right now? He shivered.

But that was ridiculous. Who would even care what he and his mother were talking about? Especially if everyone in the town had one, surely there were more interesting people to spy on than a middle-aged Polish engineer and her juvenile delinquent son. The only reason Julien had gotten on Michel's radar was because he'd been trying to hack his Lyre. Even Stan knew that was asking for trouble. Not that it justified getting beaten up. But as long as Stan didn't do anything like that, nobody would even care about what he was doing.

Even after those reassuring thoughts, it took a while

before Stan finally fell asleep that night. When he woke the next morning, his mother was once again already at work, despite having stayed so late the night before. DeCobray must be even more demanding of their employees at the headquarters than they were in the regional offices.

When Stan got to school, he stopped at the front door. There was no way he'd be able do anything in class without his Lyre device, so he somewhat reluctantly put it on. As soon as it was in place, text appeared:

NOTICE: ALL-SCHOOL ASSEMBLY IN THE AUDITORIUM DURING FIRST PERIOD.

An all-school assembly? He wondered what it was about . . .

He realized with a pang that his orientation counselor would probably not be interested in helping him anymore. Well, he'd find out soon enough.

His Lyre display guided him through the hallways to the auditorium. It was a huge theater-style space with a bare black stage. First period didn't start for another ten minutes, but a lot of the seats were already filled, with students whispering excitedly to each other. Why was anyone excited for a school assembly?

Off to one corner, Stan spotted Julien. The seat next to him was free, so he sat down beside him.

"Why's everybody so worked up?" he asked.

"Oh, hey Stan." Julien glanced at him for a moment, then went back to whatever he was looking at on his display. "People are excited because it's a school assembly."

"Yeah? And?"

"Oh right, this is your first one. Assemblies mean product updates."

"For our Lyres? What's the update?"

"They like to keep it a surprise. You know how tech companies are."

"Yeah, I guess. Are *you* excited?"

"Kind of?" Julien admitted. "On the one hand, Lyres are a mind-boggling invasion of privacy. Like, I have a hard time believing they're even legal."

"And on the other hand?" asked Stan.

"The tech is ridiculously cool."

Stan had to admit it was. And for a techie like Julien, it was probably even harder to resist.

"What do you think about joining that Average Joes club?" asked Stan.

Julien shrugged. "I think anything that keeps Zoro-me between me and Michel is a good thing."

"I know that's right," said Stan.

"Besides, what have we got to lose?"

"Well, I get the feeling that Scarlett might be looking for trouble, you know?"

Julien grinned at him. "And that's not you?"

"No, it *is* me. That's the problem," said Stan. "I promised my mom I'd be good this time. No fights, no suspensions. But if we're going to be helping out other kids who get bullied, I won't be able to help myself. I just get so *mad*, you know?"

"I don't really get angry like that. But I *do* like trouble."

"Hacker's gotta hack?" guessed Stan.

Julien looked pleased. "You know it. But seriously, are you going to join or not?

"I don't know."

"I bet if you kept your head down, you could float through the next five years pretty easily."

Stan made a face. "When you say it like that, it sounds super boring."

Julien shrugged. "If it looks like a duck and quacks like a duck . . ."

"I hear you."

Then the lights in the auditorium began to dim.

"Here we go!" whispered Julien, looking excited in spite of himself.

Quiet electronic music began to play in the background as the lights went out completely. Then a single spotlight appeared onstage with Principal Zartan. He was dressed just as dapper as yesterday, although this time it was a pale blue suit with an orange tie and pocket square.

He smiled, showing perfect white teeth. "Good morning, students of Springfield Academy!"

Everyone began cheering like it was a rock concert.

Zartan raised his hands and gestured for calm. "OK, OK, enough buttering me up. Sheesh."

The cheers died down.

"Now, we all know that online social media, Virtual Reality, even Augmented Reality are relics of the past— or rather they soon will be. Because *Extended Reality* is the way of the future!"

There were a few whoops from the audience, which Zartan didn't seem to mind.

"Exactly. Why choose between the immediacy of the real, and the flexibility of the virtual, when you can have *both*? Before smartphones, everyone was disconnected from anything outside their immediate surroundings. After smartphones, everyone was staring at their phones and disconnected from what was right in front of them. But DeCobray's Lyre XR device bridges that gap, inserting technology into your life so seamlessly, you can't even tell where one ends and the other begins."

He paused dramatically for a moment.

"You know . . . it's a little bit like magic."

Suddenly the auditorium lit up, but instead of a modern theater, it now looked like a clearing in a wooded grove. Fairies flew overhead, while little gnomes and elves scampered through nearby trees. Zartan was now dressed in a pale blue wizard robe, and the rest of the audience was also dressed in fantasy garb.

"Whether you prefer cozy fantasy or epic, with multiple configuration settings, the Magica filter is for you!" declared Zartan.

All the wizards and warriors and rogues and rangers in the audience applauded.

"But wait!" exclaimed Zartan. "What if you're more of a sci-fi person? Don't worry, we've got you covered with the new Sciffy filter!"

Now the auditorium appeared to be a vast room inside a spaceship. The walls and ceiling were all glass, so Stan could see the blackness of space stretching out all around them, with countless twinkling stars. Zartan looked like some sort of blue-skinned alien with big bug eyes. The students were a bizarre hodgepodge of blue, green, and purple. Some had antenna, others long pointy ears or snoutlike noses.

"Again, with multiple configurations, it doesn't matter whether you prefer laser swords or teleporters, you can go beyond infinity where no one has gone before, plus ultra!" said Zartan, mashing up at least three different sci-fi properties as far as Stan could tell.

All the various aliens cheered.

"I'm glad you like the two newest Lyre device filters. Please test them out and send any feedback directly to my personal in-box. I can't wait to learn what you think!"

Abruptly everything was back to normal, which Stan had to admit was kind of a letdown after the crazy visuals he'd just experienced. It had all looked so real that if Stan believed in fairies and space aliens, he might have thought it was. As everyone began to get up and go to their next period, Stan turned to Julien.

"OK, I can see why people get excited for these. That was . . ."

But Julien was still sitting, and there was a look of dread on his face.

"Julien?" asked Stan. "You OK?"

Julien looked up at him with haunted eyes.

"They pushed out two new filters to our devices without our knowledge or consent. Then they switched them on for all of us at once, also without our consent."

"Oh, yeah." Stan frowned. "I guess that's pretty invasive."

"*Invasive?*" Julien's skin was starting to look a sickly gray. "It's terrifying. Don't you realize what this means?"

"I guess not," admitted Stan.

"They can change the way anyone wearing this device perceives reality, at any time."

"But we can tell the difference," objected Stan.

"Only because they're using obvious filters like magic and sci-fi. Things we know don't exist. But what if they secretly pushed out a filter that only *subtly* changed how we see the world around us? Would we even notice?"

Finally Stan got it. "We wouldn't be able to tell the difference between what's real and what they *want* us to see."

Now the cool tech device in his ears felt even more sinister than before. His hand hovered over it, wanting to pull it off. But he still wouldn't be able to get through his classes without it. At least during school hours, they were all stuck with whatever reality Springfield Academy and DeCobray chose to show them.

OK, sure, that was scary. But Stan wondered, how bad could it really get?

A REAL EMPTY TOWN

The day's classes had been shortened to accommodate the school assembly. Yet the teachers didn't seem interested in reducing the material they wanted to cover. The morning flew by so fast that Stan could barely keep up, much less worry about what his Lyre was or was not showing him.

Since Stan and Julien were both eighth graders, they had the same lunch period. After picking up food from the cafeteria line, Stan took a seat beside his new friend.

"I can't believe how great cafeteria food is at Springfield Academy."

He eagerly picked up his bacon cheeseburger with two hands and took a big bite. It was so delicious that it was several seconds before he realized that Julien hadn't responded. He glanced over and saw that his friend looked even more freaked out than he had that morning.

"Hey, what's up?"

Julien looked gravely at him for a moment, then said, "I want to introduce you to someone."

"Sure."

Julien stood up. "Cool."

"What, like right now? Can I finish my lunch first?" he asked plaintively. It really was good.

But Julien's eyes were fixed on something else and he spoke in a low voice. "This'll only take a minute."

"OK, I guess."

Stan lovingly placed his burger back on the plate, then followed Julien over to another table where a boy with sandy blond hair sat enjoying his own bacon cheeseburger.

Suddenly, Julien's expression brightened, and he spoke in a cheery voice. "Hey, Conner, how you been?"

Conner smiled. "Hey, Julien. What's up?"

"You know, doing my thing. This is our transfer student, Stan."

"Right! The principal introduced you yesterday. Welcome to Springfield!"

"Uh, thanks." Stan wondered why Julien wanted to introduce him to this guy and why his demeanor had shifted to this weird fake cheerfulness.

"You ready for the next Smash tournament?" Julien asked Conner.

"You bet!" said Conner.

"You still maining Donkey Kong Junior?"

"Of course I am! You still maining Zelda?"

"Always and forever," said Julien.

Conner chuckled. "Well, you better get ready to lose, then."

"You wish, man. I'll see you there."

"Wouldn't miss it!" said Conner.

Still smiling, Julien led Stan back to their seats. He waited until Conner turned his focus back to eating, then his cheerful expression dropped away. He rubbed his temples, as if that had been some terrible ordeal.

"Was . . . that a weird conversation or something?" asked Stan as he started to eat again. It seemed normal enough to him, but he didn't know this Conner person, so maybe it wasn't.

"No, it was a perfectly ordinary conversation," said Julien. "I've had dozens like it with him. That's the part that worries me the most."

"What do you mean?"

"Tell your Lyre to turn off its display."

"Display off," Stan said.

A moment later, all the little peripheral information, such as date, time, and student information, disappeared.

"OK, it's off," he said.

"Look over at Conner."

Stan glanced back at Conner, who looked exactly the same. He was calmly eating his food and occasionally gesturing with his hand, so he was probably watching a video on his Lyre or something.

"O . . . kay?"

"You still see him with the display off, right?" Julien asked tensely.

"Yeah."

"Now, take *off* your Lyre."

Stan was still looking at Conner when he took the buds out of his ears. So it was easy to see the difference.

Conner wasn't there.

"What the . . ."

"You don't see him anymore, do you," said Julien.

Stan shook his head.

"OK, put them back on. I think if we keep them off too long during school hours, they'll notice."

Stan put his Lyre device back on and there was Conner again.

"I have so many questions," he said.

"No kidding," said Julien.

"First of all, he's not really there, right?"

"Right."

"How was I seeing him if I turned the display off?"

"Because the device wasn't actually off," said Julien. "It gets rid of the peripherals, but it can and apparently *does* project things even when you think it's not doing anything."

"So we were . . . talking to Conner while he's some-where else?" asked Stan. "Like video chat?"

"I really hope that's the case, but I don't think so. Why would he be *pretending* to be here?"

"So who were we talking to?"

"A really good AI version of Conner."

"An artificial intelligence that can talk video games?" asked Stan. "But how would it know about your favorite character and stuff?"

"If both of our Lyre devices have been cataloging every single conversation we've had together, an AI could come up with a pretty good guess. And that's not even the part that worries me most."

"You think he's missing, and for some reason the school is trying to hide that?"

"Missing," said Julien. "Or taken."

Up to that point, Stan still hadn't decided if he wanted to check out the Average Joes club that afternoon. But now, having some troublemaking, martial-arts-skilled friends around to watch his back sounded like a pretty good idea.

"You know, I think I'm going to join Scarlett's club after all," he said.

"Same," said Julien.

CHAPTER 8

>>>>>>> **A REAL CLUBHOUSE TOWN** >>>>>>>

Stan had assumed the club meeting would be in one of the classrooms, but when he messaged Scarlett about where to meet, she told him to find her by the soccer field behind the school.

The Springfield Vipers varsity team was warming up when Stan and Julien met Scarlett on the athletic field.

"Here, try to be discreet." She handed them each a small metallic bag like the one they'd used the night before to block the signals for their Lyres.

Stan and Julien nodded to each other, then slipped their Lyres into their bags and put them into their pockets.

"This way," said Scarlett.

They followed her to a small brick building nestled against the tree line that marked the boundary of the school grounds. It looked like it was meant to store gardening tools or something. Compared to the rest of the school, it was oddly rustic.

"This is our clubroom?" Stan asked.

"I know it looks like some kind of murder shed," said Scarlett. "But it's the only place on campus without video surveillance that we could reserve for an after-school club."

The interior was much like he expected, with creaky wooden floors, exposed brick walls, and a couple of windows that let in a feeble amount of light. There were a few chairs scattered around and a large table in the center. Zoro-me was waiting for them, his arms folded across his chest, his black hoodie pulled low over his face like always. Stan wondered if that was to look cool or if he was self-conscious about his scars. Maybe a bit of both.

"I'm glad you two decided to come," said Scarlett. "I know it's kind of a risk."

"I wasn't sure, honestly," said Stan. "The last thing I need is to get into more fights at school. But Julien figured out something today that makes me think being part of a group might be the safest thing right now."

"What did you find out?" Scarlett asked Julien.

"There's this kid in our class who *looks* like he's at school but isn't. The Lyre seems to be projecting some sort of reactive AI version of him that all students see, even when they think their displays are off."

"Yeah, Conner Peterson, right?" asked Scarlett, not looking even a little surprised. "As far as we've been able to tell, five students went missing this morning."

Stan stared at her. "You're kidding."

"I wish," said Scarlett.

"So what does this mean?" he asked.

"We have no idea," admitted Scarlett.

"Messing with our reality and spying on our messages is one thing," said Julien. "But five missing kids? That's on a whole different level."

"I agree," said Scarlett. "Finding those kids is our top priority."

"Whoa, *we're* going to find them?" asked Stan.

"Who else?" she asked plaintively.

He knew she had a point. Most students were so dazzled by all the cool tech, especially with the two new filters they just got. They were probably all wandering around magical lands or futuristic planets right now. And maybe that wasn't a coincidence. Maybe whoever took the students had timed it to coincide with the Lyre update. So those kids were missing, and nobody even noticed . . .

Anastasia had accused Stan of having some kind of hero complex. And maybe that was true in some way, because he knew he couldn't turn a blind eye to this.

"I'm in," he said.

"Me too," said Julien.

"I can't promise you won't get in trouble with the school," said Scarlett. "Are you sure?"

"If I didn't try to do something about this, I'd be having nightmares tonight," said Julien.

Stan thought about his father. What would *he* have done?

"Yeah," he told Scarlett. "I'm sure."

She nodded gravely. "Then welcome to the Average Joes club. Let's go help some people."

A REAL SECURE TOWN ››››››››››

Scarlett led them back to the school, then down into the basement, which didn't have the same slick-looking glass and chrome appearance as the rest of the school. The floor was plain cement, and the space was partitioned into storage areas with chain-link walls. There were stacks of folding tables, chairs, and neat piles of sports equipment. None of them had their phones to light the way, so Scarlett flicked on a small pocket flashlight.

"Zoro-me has been keeping an eye on Michel and

Anastasia's movements," Scarlett said quietly as her narrow beam of light bounced with her footsteps. "They seem to come down here a lot, sometimes even during class."

Finally they reached a steel door at the far end.

"This is where they go." She shined her light on a keypad beside the door. "Using that."

"I don't suppose you were able to see what they were typing?" asked Stan.

Zoro-me shook his head.

"But," said Scarlett, "we think there's another way through."

"Where?" asked Stan.

She moved the light up to a narrow vent cover above the door.

They stared at it in silence for a moment.

"Someone has to squeeze through there?" asked Stan.

Scarlett nodded, her eyes on him. Zoro-me and Julien also seemed to look at him expectantly.

Stan's eyes narrowed. "You want *me* to do it?"

Scarlett gave him a pained smile. "You *are* the smallest."

He sighed. "Fine. You guys are lucky I'm not claustro-phobic or anything."

"We are," agreed Scarlett.

He squared his shoulders and nodded. "OK, let's get it over with."

Zoro-me stood under the vent, then Scarlett jumped onto his shoulders with startling agility.

"Whoa, are you a gymnast?" Stan asked.

She nodded as she began unscrewing the vent. "Practically since I could walk."

"I'm so jealous," said Julien.

"Why?" asked Stan.

"Man, I have zero athletic ability. I'm so clumsy, if I tried to hop up on Zoro-me's shoulders like that, I'd prob-ably end up breaking *both* our necks."

Once Scarlett had the cover off, she jumped gracefully back.

She handed him the tiny flashlight. "All yours, Stan."

"Right." He looked at Zoro-me. He was fairly coordi-nated, but he didn't think he could do what Scarlett had done. "Uh . . . maybe a boost?"

Zoro-me nodded and laced his fingers together. Stan stepped into his hands, and Zoro-me boosted him up with relative ease.

Stan peered into the shaft. All he saw was a narrow, metal passage that disappeared into the darkness.

"Here we go," he muttered, then clenched the flashlight between his teeth, pushed off Zoro-me's hands, and scrambled into the vent.

But only halfway. His feet scrabbled uselessly against the wall, and as he pressed his hands against the smooth sides of the shaft, he felt himself slowly sliding back.

"Halp!" he said around the flashlight, and wiggled his feet.

A moment later, he felt several pairs of hands grab his ankles and push him all the way into the vent.

He lay there for a moment in the darkness, his breath whistling around the flashlight. The metal seemed to press in all around, and every time he moved it sounded like a timpani drum. The air was stuffy and dry, and he could feel a tickle of panic at the back of his throat. He'd never thought of himself as claustrophobic, but he'd also never tried to shove himself into such a tight, dark space before.

"You OK, Stan?" Scarlett's voice called.

He took the flashlight out of his mouth and swallowed. "Yeah. I'm OK."

It was slow going as he crawled along the narrow shaft. His eyes watered from the dust, and his knees were getting bruised from repeatedly banging into the metal. The passage was probably no more than ten feet long, but it seemed to take forever for him to get to the other side.

Once he got there, he realized there was a vent covering the other side. Because, of course, there would be.

"Huh."

Stan took a slow breath, determined to keep the tremors of panic at bay. Awkwardly, he shifted around in the narrow shaft until his feet were in front of him. This was what they did in the movies, wasn't it? They kicked it out.

He gave the cover a good, hard kick.

It hurt. A lot.

He bit down on his lip to keep from crying out, then craned his neck so he could look around his knees.

The vent was still totally intact.

What was he going to do? He was stuck up here, in this small, hot, airless space . . .

He took another slow deep breath. He was fine. If worse came to worse, he could just crawl back the way he came and rejoin the others, feeling a little sheepish but otherwise unharmed.

He spun back around to face the vent and examined it carefully with the flashlight. He felt it with his hands, testing for weak spots. The corners were screwed in securely. He wasn't going to kick those out. But he noticed that the metal slats in the middle of the vent were thin, and actually pretty flimsy.

Once more he shifted around until he was feet first. Instead of using his whole foot, he flexed it so it was heel first. Then he started kicking in the middle of the slats. This time, he didn't do it as hard as he could. Instead, he was more focused on accuracy. Hitting in the same spot, over and over again.

Slowly, the slats began to buckle until finally they split down the middle. He'd broken through.

Sort of. Now it was a bunch of spiky metal tines that

looked very sharp. So still using his feet, which were protected by his leather sneakers, he pressed the tines back and away until at last there was a hole big enough for him to get through without getting stabbed.

Once he'd jumped down on the other side, he looked around the space. He'd expected it to be a room of some kind, but instead it was a narrow hallway that terminated at an elevator.

He found the door that led back to his friends and pushed it open.

"I'm basically a spy now," he told them.

Scarlett grinned. "I'm sure that will come in handy. So what's the room back there like?"

"Oh, it's not a room," he said. "Just a hallway with an elevator."

"An elevator?" she asked sharply.

"Yeah," said Stan. "And it only goes down."

"That doesn't make any sense," she said.

"See for yourself." He stepped aside so they could enter.

Once they were all inside, Scarlett chewed worriedly on her lip as she stared at the closed elevator door. "There must be a subbasement, I guess."

Stan pressed the button, but it didn't light up. Then he noticed the small plastic plate beside it.

"Oh no, I think we need to scan some kind of card or fob for it to work. We had one like that for our apartment building back in Chicago."

"Man, a fob scanner? That's kid's stuff." Julien shook his head as he pulled out a smartphone that he was definitely not supposed to have on campus. "Observe."

He pressed the back of his contraband phone against the scanner, then ran some kind of weird coding app on his phone.

"You think biometrics would have been more secure?" asked Scarlett.

"Depends," said Julien. "I could spoof your thumbprint with a gummy bear. And retinal scanners aren't much better. Only something like a full-face or voice scan would be an actual challenge."

"I guess we're lucky they didn't use that, then," said Stan.

"Probably not luck," said Julien. "If more than a few people needed to pass through here, or if it's connected to a large network of security systems, it would be cost-prohibitive to install a bunch of full-face scanners just to lock down some elevators that were already secured behind a keypad door."

His phone beeped quietly. He pressed the elevator down button, and this time it lit up.

"And there we go!"

"It's a good thing we have you here," said Scarlett.

"It is." The elevator doors opened, and Julien gestured dramatically. "After you."

A REAL POLITE TOWN

A man sat at a bank of monitors, his hands steepled together. There were fifty monitors in all, each displaying footage from four cameras, a total of two hundred viewpoints at once. The images changed every thirty seconds, showing a different two hundred cameras each time. It cycled through several sets before returning to the original two hundred.

It would have been impossible to carefully observe what was being recorded by every camera. But the man didn't need to do that. He had perfected a skill that allowed him to sweep his gaze across the entire collage of images, and his eyes would be automatically drawn to anything that was unusual, furtive, or suspicious. If something caught his attention, he could lock on to that particular camera with a single tap of his control panel, bringing it forward and out of the regular cycle.

He had been watching one camera for several minutes.

On the screen were three boys and a girl. Facial recognition software identified them as users registered in the Lyre XR database, with ages ranging from thirteen to sixteen. They were talking animatedly to each other, looking very pleased with themselves for having circumvented the paltry scanner control for the elevator system.

He checked the camera location. Springfield Academy basement.

"Hmmm," he said in a languorous, almost lazy voice. "Interesting."

The door burst open and a soldier dressed in a blue-and-black uniform with a red cobra insignia on the chest stepped into the room.

"Commander!" He saluted sharply. "There's been a security breach at—"

Without taking his eyes off the screen, the Commander tapped his console.

The soldier halted, his eyes wide with terror as the tiny light on his Lyre device flickered rapidly.

Then his head exploded.

"It's considered polite to knock before entering a room," the Commander said absently. Then he steepled his hands once more and watched as the four teenagers stepped into the elevator, and the doors slid closed behind them.

"*Very* interesting," he said.

CHAPTER

11

A REAL MAD SCIENCE TOWN

Stan didn't know what he'd expected to see when the elevator doors opened. But it definitely wasn't a subway station.

The elevator seemed to open onto an underground platform similar to the platforms Stan associated with the L back in Chicago. Next to the platform was a line of tracks that disappeared into a dark tunnel. There was even a sign on the wall that read:

SPRINGFIELD ACADEMY
STATION

"So, uh . . ." said Stan, "did anybody else know that Springfield had a subway system?"

"Nope," Scarlett said quietly. "And I've lived here my whole life. This is bigger than I realized. Maybe we should—"

Then there was a muffled scream. It was a long, drawn out, painful sound. Like someone was about to be murdered.

"This way!" said Scarlett.

She ran down the platform, with Stan and the others following behind. At the far end of the platform was a thick wooden door. The scream was coming from the other side.

Scarlett reached for the door, but Zoro-me put his hand across it and shook his head.

She stood there a moment with her hand hovering, like she was fighting against her own instincts. Then she closed her eyes and took a deep breath.

"You're right, Zoro-me. We can't just go in blind, or we might make things worse."

He nodded and tapped his chest.

"OK, scout ahead. We'll wait here for you."

Zoro-me opened the door soundlessly; then he was gone.

It was terrible standing there, helpless, while they listened to those terrified screams. Sometimes the sounds were sharp, and sometimes they were more like long whimpers or moans. Stan had never heard a person make noises like that before, and it wrenched at his heart.

"Whatever is going on inside," said Scarlett, "we have to make sure we don't get recognized. Right now, even if they suspect we're causing a little trouble in school, they aren't going to bother with us. But if they catch us down here, I'm pretty sure that'll be the end of our club. And maybe us. Understood?"

They nodded.

After several more agonizing moments of listening to screams, the door opened again. Zoro-me was crouched low. He motioned to the rest of them to do the same, then he tapped his finger to his lips and went back inside.

They followed him in a low crouch down an aisle. There were rows of shelves on either side filled with test tubes, weird gadgets, and bottles of liquids and powders labeled with long, complicated chemical names like "flunitrazepam" and "3-Quinuclidinyl benzilate." Maybe the horrible screaming in the background was coloring his perception, but it seemed to Stan like the storage room for an evil mad scientist.

Beyond the shelves was an open area, and then a row of four doors, each with a large bay window next to it. Stan could see tiny rooms like prison cells on the other side of each window. One room contained a tall thin girl who was huddled in the corner, screaming her lungs out like a monster was about to attack her, but there was no one else in the room. Another room contained two boys who were fighting each other, but not like kids normally fight. They were almost like wild animals, biting and scratching each other bloody and raw, their clothes torn to shreds. One of those boys looked like Conner. In the third room was a girl who was laughing uncontrollably. In the fourth, a boy was sobbing hysterically.

Principal Zartan and Michel stood in front of the window that showed the girl screaming in terror. Instead of a suit, the principal was dressed in a white lab coat with a strange red logo on the breast pocket that looked like a cobra with its hood open. He watched the girl with keen interest, his hands darting in front of him, clearly doing something with his Lyre. Michel just looked bored.

After a few moments, Zartan opened the door to the screaming girl's cell. He stood in the doorway and said something to her, but she didn't seem to notice because she was too busy shrieking in terror. He nodded in satisfaction, then closed the door again and adjusted something on his Lyre display.

The whole thing truly was like out of a mad scientist horror movie, with Stan's own principal as the villain. He could barely take it in, much less come up with some kind of plan for what to do about it.

Thankfully, Scarlett was there. She tapped them each on the shoulder, and they tore their eyes away from the horrible sight. Once she had their attention, she held up one finger, pointed to Julien, then pointed to a nearby light switch. She held up two fingers, pointed to Zoro-me, then pointed to Zartan and Michel. She held up three fingers, pointed to Stan, then pointed to the first two doors. Finally, she held up four fingers, pointed to herself, then pointed to the other two doors. So Julien would hit the lights, then Zoro-me would somehow distract Zartan and

Michel. In the darkness and confusion, Stan and Scarlett would try to free the kids.

It wasn't a complicated plan, but she had come up with it on the spot in this stressful moment and explained it in complete silence in a way that they all immediately understood. This, Stan decided, was what real leadership looked like.

She gestured for Julien to begin edging around the storage shelves over to the light switch, then held up her hand to indicate that they would start on her signal.

Zartan swiped something on his Lyre display and frowned.

"It's certainly a *strong* reaction," he muttered to himself. "But is it *useful*? He'll expect implementation strategies, of course . . ."

"Say, boss, are you almost done?" asked Michel. "These kids are giving me a headache."

"Patience, Mr. LeClerc, patience." Zartan's eyes remained on the screaming girl. "You cannot rush genius."

"Uh-huh." Michel did not seem impressed. "You could have at least sprung for some soundproofing."

After a few moments, Zartan tapped something on his Lyre display, and abruptly all the students stopped freaking out. The scared girl seemed to realize she was alone; the two fighting boys seemed suddenly to question why they were fighting and then looked in horror at the injuries they'd inflicted on each other. The girl who had been laughing began gasping for air, as though she'd barely been breathing the whole time. And the sad boy suddenly snapped out of his misery, only to find he was trapped in a completely different unpleasant situation from whatever he had been seeing before.

By that time, Julien had finally reached the light switch on the far wall. Scarlett looked like she was about to signal, but then Michel said something that made her pause.

"So, when are we bringing them back up to the school?"

Zartan looked at him in surprise. "Bring them back? Oh no, I think they'll be quite ruined by the time we're done with them."

"OK, let me ask a different question," said Michel without batting an eye. "What am I supposed to do with the bodies?"

"That's hardly my area of expertise, Mr. LeClerc."

Scarlett dropped her hand.

Julien cut the lights.

"What the—" began Zartan before Zoro-me knocked his feet out from under him. Michel reacted quickly, lunging in the dark for Zoro-me, but Zoro-me dodged, and delivered a swift counter.

Stan would have loved to continue watching Zoro-me's incredible combat skills, but he tore himself away and moved quickly through the dark to the doors. He yanked one open, wondering if they were locked only on the inside, or maybe not even locked at all. The terrified girl was so disoriented now that there was no way she could have escaped on her own. Fortunately, because she was so out of it, she did whatever Stan said, and he was able to hurry her out of the room without fuss.

Zoro-me was still somehow fighting both Zartan and Michel at once, but Stan didn't know how much longer he could keep that up, so he hastily pulled open the door with the two boys.

They looked at him in baffled incomprehension.

"Hurry!" he shouted. "This way!"

"What's going on?" demanded Conner.

"No time, Conner! You have to come now!"

The other boy eagerly hurried over to him, and after a moment of hesitation, Conner did as well. They gaped at the barely visible struggle and sounds of fighting in the dark hallways, but Stan urged them over to the storage shelves where Scarlett and Julien waited with the other students.

"Time to go!" Scarlett shouted.

Stan pushed the students after her. "Go! Go!"

He was about to follow them when he felt a hand grab his ankle.

"Oh no you don't!" he heard Michel growl.

Stan lost his balance and pitched forward into the storage shelves, knocking over a whole line of bottles with a loud crash. He didn't know what was in the bottles, but a moment later he heard glass shatter, then Michel let out a wail of pain and released his ankle.

Stan felt terrible. Even though Michel was clearly an awful person, there was a difference in his mind between punching someone in the face and causing whatever horrible pain had just befallen Michel.

Maybe a chemical burn? But he knew he had to use this chance to escape while the lights were still out.

Scarlett, Julien, and the other students were already out of the room. Stan raced for the door that led back to the subway platform, but he was still about twelve feet away when it opened, revealing Anastasia.

"Why are the lights out?" demanded Anastasia.

"Stop them!" shouted Zartan from behind. "Whoever they are, catch them!"

Stan jerked to a halt. He was still in the dark, so she hadn't spotted him yet. But his escape was cut off. He was trapped. He had only seconds before they found him. What should he do?

Then he felt a hand grip his mouth.

CHAPTER 12

>>>>>>>>>> IS IT REALLY A TOWN? >>>>>>>>>>

The hand that gripped Stan's mouth was incredibly strong. And then in a series of lightning-quick motions, the person knocked his legs out from under him, caught him before he hit the ground, then rolled him under the nearest shelf.

Stan figured there was only one person who could move that fast, and a moment later his suspicion was confirmed when Zoro-me rolled under the shelf beside him.

"I don't see anyone," said Anastasia as she squinted into the dark room.

"They're here! They must be!" snapped Zartan. "Where is that blasted light switch . . ."

Zoro-me looked over at Stan and tapped his lips, as if Stan really needed the reminder to stay silent. Then Zoro-me reached up, took a bottle from the shelf above them, and tossed it so that it broke closer to where Zartan and Michel were.

Anastasia grinned. "Got you!"

She ran past, then Zoro-me and Stan scrambled out from under the shelf and hurried through the door back to the subway platform. Stan didn't see the others, so hopefully they'd already escaped up the elevator.

Behind him, Stan heard Zartan shout, "No, you fool! They must have slipped past you! They're on the plat-form! Go! Go!"

Zoro-me and Stan sprinted toward the elevator. But as they got closer, Stan saw that the elevator doors were now closed. There was a security pad on this side, too, and they didn't have the hacker tool that Julien used to open it.

Then Stan heard the unmistakable rumble of a subway car about to enter the station.

Zoro-me grabbed Stan's arm and nodded to the tracks.

Stan could already see the train headlights glaring in the subway tunnel.

"Whatever you're thinking, it's a terrible idea . . ." he said to Zoro-me.

Zoro-me looked to where Anastasia and Michel, who was clutching the side of his face and looking absolutely murderous, were just emerging from the mad science lab.

"Well, yeah, I guess it's not any worse, but—"

Zoro-me took that as a yes, grabbed Stan by the shirt, and rolled them both off the platform and across the first rail so that they lay between the tracks. A moment later, the train rattled over them and came to a halt with a hydraulic hiss.

Stan thought they would lay there until the train left and the coast was clear, but as soon as the train stopped, Zoro-me wiggled up the narrow gap between the tracks until he reached a junction between cars, then climbed up. Stan followed with a lot less ease, managing to lose part of his shirt and a bit of skin. Zoro-me helped him up, and once they stood on the narrow joint between cars, he gave him a reassuring pat on the shoulder.

"Thanks," Stan said dryly.

Stan peered into the cars on either side. They were both full of normal-looking adults in regular business clothes. They didn't *seem* like mad scientists or evil henchmen, but if they were on this secret subway train, surely they had to be connected to Zartan somehow. Although he noticed they all wore Lyre devices, so maybe they were seeing something totally different.

"We should probably stay out of sight, just in case," he whispered.

Zoro-me nodded.

They crouched down so passengers couldn't see them through the windows. A moment later the train started up again, and they had to cling to the door handles for dear life while it zoomed through the tunnel.

Thankfully it was only a few minutes before the train slowed to a stop at a platform labeled Red Rocket Station. A few people got off, and then just as the train was starting to move again, Zoro-me tapped Stan and they both jumped onto the platform.

The train zoomed away. The few people who had gotten off were already far ahead and didn't see them. They hung back behind a pillar as the people walked to the end of the platform where there was another elevator identical to the one at Springfield Academy Station.

Except this elevator was guarded by two men with machine guns. They were dressed in dark blue uniforms and helmets, with black masks that covered their mouths and noses. The front of their uniforms was emblazoned with the same red cobra symbol that had been on Zartan's lab coat.

The businesspeople filed past the guards one at a time. Either they weren't bothered by the weird paramilitary uniforms, or their Lyre devices were showing them something completely different.

Once all the people had gone up the elevator, Zoro-me indicated for Stan to stay put. Then he pulled his hood down extra low and stepped out into view.

Stan watched in amazement as Zoro-me casually walked up to the two guards. They seemed confused at first. They probably weren't used to random teenagers showing up there. It looked like they asked him for something. One of them tapped their Lyre device. That's probably how they could tell who belonged and who didn't.

Zoro-me only stood there looking at them.

That seemed to make them mad, but just as they began to raise their weapons, Zoro-me did his thing, and a moment later, they were somehow both on the ground, unconscious. Zoro-me stooped over and retrieved a key card from one of them, then motioned for Stan to join him.

Stan jogged up the platform while Zoro-me tapped the card on the elevator key panel and hit the up button.

"Zoro-me . . ." Stan looked in awe at his friend, who had just taken out two heavily armed guards like it was no big deal. "How are you so *amazing*??"

Zoro-me shrugged and said, "I'm shinobi."

Of course, thought Stan. He'd had it all wrong. The dojo wasn't like an old samurai film. The Arashikages were a family of freaking *ninjas*.

A REAL SHINOBI TOWN

The elevator let them out inside the Red Rocket diner. The platform sign had clued Stan in on that, but it was still such an abrupt shift that he stood there blinking in the bright, modern lightning. Then Zoro-me tapped his arm and nodded toward the exit.

"Yeeeah, good call," said Stan.

They walked as casually as they could through the diner, and somehow no one noticed their torn clothes and smudged faces. Or maybe they just pretended not to notice. Or maybe their Lyre devices made Stan and Zoro-me look like giant pandas. Who even knew at this point. Stan had decided that he couldn't take anything for granted in this town.

Once they were back out on the sidewalk, it felt weird to look around at this "Real American Town" and know that there was something very sinister going on underneath.

"Should we go back to the school clubroom?" he asked Zoro-me.

Zoro-me shook his head and motioned for him to follow. Stan wasn't that surprised when he saw that their destination was the Arashikage Dojo.

"Yeah, this might actually be the safest place in town for us," he said.

Zoro-me nodded.

As soon they stepped through the door, Scarlett rushed over to Zoro-me.

"Okaerinasai," she whispered, and hugged him fiercely.

Stan stood awkwardly beside them as the two held the embrace.

"You want a hug, Stan?" offered Julien from where he

sat on a cushion with a steaming mug of what looked like hot chocolate.

"Thanks, I'm good." Stan plopped down beside his friend. He suddenly felt completely wiped out. Like he'd been running on adrenaline this whole time and now that he was somewhere safe, it had finally given out.

At last Scarlett released Zoro-me. "What happened to you guys?"

"Zoro-me saved my butt is what happened," said Stan.

She gave him a weary smile. "Don't feel bad. He saves everyone's butt."

"I did notice that was a pattern," said Stan. "What about you guys? And where are the other students?"

"We didn't want to risk the school nurse's office, in case they were working for Zartan," said Scarlett. "So we dropped them off at the hospital emergency room. It's just down the street from the school."

"We decided not to stick around though," said Julien. "Just in case."

"In case of what?" asked Stan.

But before either of them could answer, Tommy suddenly appeared. By this point, Stan wasn't even surprised. Really, if he was going to hang out in a ninja dojo, he kind of had to expect it.

"Wow, you four look like you've really been through some stuff. Average Joes club in full swing, huh?" Then his tone grew unexpectedly grave. "Seriously, Shana, what have you been doing? There's a lot of buzz right now."

"Zartan took some kids, so we got them back," she told him flatly.

His eyes widened. "I'm sorry. You did *what*?"

Scarlett looked away. "I don't want to hear it, Tommy."

"Wait. You're telling me that they *know* about us?"

"No, of course not. Give me some credit."

"But they know that *somebody* in town has wised up."

Scarlett threw her hands up. "What did you want me to do—leave those poor kids to Zartan's freaky experiments?"

Tommy's face creased with anger. "Yes, that's *exactly* what you should have done. You brought these two in, fine. Julien has a useful skill set, and my brother thinks Stan has combat potential, so I guess I can go along with it. But risking everything for some *randos*?"

"Nobody's just a rando!" objected Stan.

But Tommy was so focused on Scarlett, he didn't seem to hear. As he spoke, he emphasized his words with a pointed finger. "If they know that they're losing control of people, they will tighten everything up. That puts you, me, my brother, and everybody else in jeopardy. Worse, it puts the *masters' goals* in jeopardy. Is that what you want?"

"Of course not, Tommy."

"Don't forget, you were miserable and alone when we got here. The masters took you in, trained you, welcomed you into our home. They treat you like *family*. Does that mean anything to you?

"You know it does!" Scarlett's face twisted with conflicting emotions. "But I can't just—"

"Yes, you can!" His face was now flush with anger. "If these kids were taken, it's because they're weak, and you are better off without them!"

"Hey!"

Stan had heard enough.

"Tommy, why are you such a jerk?"

Tommy turned, and there was now a terrifying coldness in his expression that reminded Stan way too much of Hādo. His voice also switched to a quiet murmur that was far more intimidating than when he'd been shouting at Scarlett.

"I knew you were a stupid eighth grader, but I didn't realize you were *that* stupid. When *I* do something stupid, my uncle beats the lesson into me. Maybe I should do the same for you."

"You think I'm scared of you?" He was, actually. Deeply scared. But Tommy's mentality of ignoring people who needed help upset him more than anything. "Bring your worst."

Tommy struck so fast that Stan didn't even see it coming. He should have been knocked to the ground instantly.

But he wasn't. Instead, Tommy's fist hovered inches from Stan's face, stopped by Zoro-me.

"Stay out of this, brother," growled Tommy.

Zoro-me shook his head.

"Fine!" Tommy pivoted toward him. "Then show me what the Hard Master's *favored pupil* can really do."

Stan could barely follow what happened next, partly

because it was so fast and partly because it was so *quiet*. He didn't hear the usual smack of knuckles on flesh, grunts, panting, and scuffling of feet. Their fists and feet darted in and out in a flurry of movement, yet they appeared to be so evenly matched that neither of them were able to connect a hit. It was almost like a chess game, where they feigned, and double feigned, delivering a seemingly clumsy strike to make it look like they were leaving themselves open, except it was only to lure the other one into leaving himself open. Except the other one saw through that and countered the counter.

Then, just as Stan was beginning to think it wasn't a real fight and the brothers were merely flexing, Zoro-me must have miscalculated something. Maybe he'd leaned a little too far forward or not angled his feet exactly right? Stan had no idea. But suddenly his friend flew backward across the room and smashed through one of the screens.

Tommy dashed forward, his eyes blazing, looking for all the world like he fully intended to kill his own brother.

Then Hādo appeared before him, his deadly presence filling the room. He lifted one hand, palm facing out. It looked like he only tapped Tommy lightly on the chest, but Tommy was knocked back and barely managed to keep his footing.

Behind Hādo, Zoro-me jumped up from the wreckage of the screen, but before he could do anything, Yawarakai was there, still smiling as he twisted Zoro-me's arm into a painful-looking hold.

"Brothers do not fight each other," Hādo said in a voice as dark and heavy as the bottom of the sea.

"Most certainly not," said Yawarakai.

"But Shujin . . ." objected Tommy. "He—"

"It does not matter," Hādo cut him off. "What's done is done, and further foolishness will not change that fact."

Tommy's face contorted with conflict for a moment, then he bowed. "My deepest apologies for my poor behavior."

Hādo's eyes swept the room until they stopped at Scarlett. "You have done enough for one day, Shana-chan. Take your club and go."

Scarlett bowed. "At once, Hādo-sensei. Thank you as always for your hospitality." Then she turned to the others. "Let's leave the Arashikage family to their evening."

CHAPTER 14

>>>>>>>>>>>>> **A REAL SHARING TOWN** >>>>>>>>>>>

There was an awkward moment as Stan, Julien, and Scarlett gathered on the sidewalk in front of the Arashikage Dojo. Stan didn't think they had been permanently banned from the dojo. At least he *hoped* not. But regardless, they had clearly annoyed Zoro-me's uncles.

"So," Scarlett said finally. "Tommy may be a jerk, but he's not wrong about one thing: We've stirred up the snake den. Even if they couldn't identify us, we're going to have to be a lot more careful going forward."

"It's funny you said 'snake den,'" said Stan. "Did you see that red snake logo on Zartan's lab coat? Zoro-me and I ran into these guards who had the same thing on their uniforms."

"The cobra logo?" she asked. "As in De-Cobra-y?"

Stan gave her a skeptical look. "Would they really be that obvious about it?"

"I mean, why not?" said Julien. "When they can make it look any way they want for most people."

"Good point," admitted Stan. "But still . . . how could DeCobray be behind all this? My mom is always going on about how amazing they are. How much they're helping people. And she was saying that *before* she got to Springfield and started wearing a Lyre."

"It wouldn't be the first time a corporation did shady things behind their employees' backs," said Scarlett. "Remember that candy company that was in the news because people found out they were getting their chocolate ingredients from places that used child slave labor?

DeCobray is a huge, multinational corporation. They could be doing all kinds of stuff we don't know about. Or they could have a front organization with its own employees, and these Cobra people are working behind the scenes. Or they could even be a totally separate organization, and Zartan is working for both companies, stealing tech from DeCobray and repurposing it for this other Cobra company."

"Couldn't it just be Zartan doing this on his own?" asked Stan.

"It's possible," said Scarlett. "But remember he said something about needing to come up with implementation strategies for someone. Like he has some boss that he answers to."

"Oh yeah, that's right . . ." There had been so much going on in that mad science lab, Stan had completely forgotten such a minor detail. It really was amazing how Scarlett was able to keep a cool head in situations like that.

But now she sighed, looking a little frustrated. "There's just so much we don't know."

"What about the kids we rescued?" asked Stan. "They should at least be able to get Zartan in trouble, right?"

"They were still pretty disoriented when we dropped them off," Scarlett said. "I'm not sure how much they even remember."

"If the Lyre devices can mess with your emotions, there's no telling what else they can do," said Julien.

"Make them forget things, even?" asked Scarlett.

Julien shrugged. "Heck if I know. I'm a computer hacker, not a brain hacker."

Stan groaned. "I wish we could just tell everyone to get rid of their Lyre devices."

"Man, that would be like telling people to toss their smartphones," said Julien. "It would take pretty compelling evidence to convince people to ditch the most amazing tech they've ever had."

"Maybe instead we could . . ." said Scarlett.

"What?" Stan asked eagerly.

She shook her head. "I may have an idea, but I need to think about it some more. I'll let you know. In the meantime, we should probably head home. Where do you two live?"

"I live on Main and Hama Street," said Stan.

"For real?" asked Julien. "I'm over at Dixon just off Main."

"That makes sense," said Scarlett. "DeCobray usually houses its people in the same general part of town. And it's a good thing for us. We can't say for certain whether Zartan and Michel recognized us. It'll be safer if you walk home together."

"What about you?" asked Stan.

She grinned. "I grew up here *and* I hang out at a ninja dojo. Nobody's going to find me if I don't want them to."

"Girl's got a point," said Julien.

"All right, I guess we'll see you tomorrow," said Stan.

"You bet," said Scarlett. "Remember, for now we have to act like everything is normal. Wear your Lyre devices at school, and keep in mind it might be showing you things that aren't real. If you see any of the kids we rescued, ask them if they remember anything, but don't pressure them. We'll meet up after school at the clubhouse to decide our next course of action."

Stan and Julien said goodbye to Scarlett and started walking home.

"I wonder if she's always that intense," said Julien.

"Scarlett?" asked Stan. "I thought you two knew each other pretty well."

"Kinda," said Julien. "I mean, my folks and I moved here about a year and a half ago when my dad got a job with DeCobray, and she's always looked out for me, like a big sister or something. But we didn't really hang out until recently, when Michel started hassling me."

"I guess she's the only one who's originally from here."

"You heard what Tommy said, right?" asked Julien. "About how she used to be miserable and alone? I wonder what he meant by that."

"It's kind of hard to imagine," said Stan. "She's always so in charge. You saw how she handled that crazy situation with Zartan."

"Totally cool and in control," agreed Julien. "But I guess we all got stuff in our past."

Stan thought about his father's death and the years that followed. The hurt. The helpless anger. "Yeah. I guess we do."

"Your mom works for DeCobray, too?" asked Julien.

"Back at their regional office in Chicago for years. And then I was having some . . . problems at school, so when my mom saw this promotion to headquarters, she took it. She said the change would do us both some good."

Julien's eyebrow rose. "I assume the 'problem' was the fighting you mentioned this morning?"

Stan nodded.

"I mean, speaking purely selfishly here, I'm kinda lucky you like to pick fights."

"I don't *like* it, though," said Stan. "I just . . ."

"You get mad."

"Yeah."

They walked in silence for a little while through the streets of Springfield. The sky was changing from orange to purple, and stars were just beginning to peek out.

"You always been like that?" asked Julien. There was no judgment in his voice, though.

"No, it was . . ."

Stan hesitated. He'd never told anyone this before. The kids back in Chicago had just *known*. The whole neighborhood had. It was one of the reasons it had been so hard to leave. Because there had been an understanding. Not here, though. But maybe Julien . . .

He glanced over at his friend, who was just walking along beside him, not pressing, not assuming. Stan had only known him for a day, he realized. And yet, he felt so easy around him. Maybe some friendships were just natural like that. It probably helped that they'd already shared some pretty crazy experiences.

"It was two years ago," he said at last. "Someone was getting mugged. My dad tried to help that person. And the mugger . . . killed him."

"Whoa . . ." Julien's eyes widened.

"I didn't see it happen, but that's what the cops told us." He clenched his fists as he pictured their hard, impassive faces. "Then as the cops were walking away, one said to the other that my dad shouldn't have done it. That it had been a stupid thing to do and he'd gotten himself killed for no reason."

"That's horrible."

"I don't think they realized I could hear them."

"Even still."

"Yeah," said Stan.

They walked a little farther.

"Say," said Julien, "you want to come over for dinner?"

"Uh, sure." Then Stan's eyes narrowed. "Wait, this isn't because you feel bad for me, is it?"

"What? No!"

"Uh-huh." Julien was still a terrible liar, but Stan appreciated the effort.

"OK, maybe that's what made me think of it," admitted Julien. "But I don't actually have many friends, and you just shared something big with me. So I felt like the least I could do is offer you the hospitality of the March household."

Stan thought about the microwave dinner that awaited him because his mom was probably working late again, and said, "I'll take it."

"Oh, just a heads-up, my mom is a good cook. But, uh, she's also a little kooky."

"Kooky?"

"You'll see."

A REAL FAMILY TOWN

The outside of Julien's house looked much like Stan's, but the inside was very different. While the Migda house was hardly furnished, with empty wooden floors and unadorned white walls, the March house was crammed full of furniture, with lush rugs on the floors and richly colored paintings crowding the walls.

And then there was the music. When they first walked in, Stan assumed someone was playing a stereo really loudly. Some sort of wild, jazzy piano number. But then Julien called out, "I'm home!" and the music cut off mid-note.

A moment later, a middle-aged woman with brown skin and long flowing black hair who was dressed in an oversize white button-up shirt came sweeping out of one of the rooms.

"My baby has come home!" She raised her hands like she was praying. "At long last!"

Julien didn't look amused. "Hi, Mom. Sorry, our, uh, school club meeting went long. This is Stan. Can he stay for dinner?"

"Perhaps . . ." She narrowed her eyes as she looked at Stan. "Are you a *polite* boy, Stan?"

"Yes, Ms. March."

"Well said. How do you feel about tofu?"

"Depends on what it's with."

"Wise answer." She nodded, looking impressed. "And lastly, what's your take on Sun Ra's seminal album *Jazz in Silhouette*?"

"Huh?"

She rolled her eyes. "Well, two out of three ain't bad. Fine, the two of you go wash up, then get ready to feast!"

She spun on her heel and swept off toward the kitchen.

Julien shrugged. "See what I mean? A little kooky."

"Who's Sun Ra?" asked Stan.

"Never mind."

While they waited for dinner, Julien showed Stan his computer setup, with two monitors, a PC tower, keyboard, and mouse that all swirled rainbow LED lights. There was also a huge chair that looked like it should have been on a rocket ship.

"A gamer's paradise," Julien said proudly.

"How did you get all this?" Stan wasn't that into video games, but he had to admit it looked impressive.

Julien looked a little embarrassed. "I think my dad felt guilty for moving us out of Kansas City for his job. So with his new DeCobray salary, I got this rig, and my mom got the grand piano she's always wanted."

"Piano?" asked Stan. "That wasn't a recording when we came in, then? That was your mom playing?"

"Yeah, she's a jazz musician."

"Is she, like, famous?"

He shrugged. "If you're a big jazz fan, I guess. She's

won a few awards, and sometimes she goes on tour and stuff."

"Whoa." Stan couldn't imagine having a parent who was famous. Even if it was only jazz famous.

"It's really not a big deal," Julien assured him. "And having an artist for a parent means things are always a little weird."

"I don't mind weird," Stan said.

"Glad to hear it. Because you're about to eat dinner with my mom."

As they sat down to dinner, Stan wondered if Julien was just exaggerating, or maybe overly embarrassed. Ms. March seemed like a totally normal mom, making sure they had enough food on their plates, that they were using napkins, and other regular parent things. The food was a little unusual. Some sort of tofu stir-fry with noodles. But it wasn't too spicy.

"So, Stan," Ms. March said once they began eating. "What do you think of Springfield so far?"

"Oh, uh . . ."

He thought back to his initial impression of the city.

Like some sort of tech utopia. Now, it seemed more like a nightmare dystopia. But he probably couldn't say that. There was really only one thing that he *could* say that was true.

"I miss Chicago," he said honestly.

"Oh, yes, a *wonderful* city," agreed Ms. March. "Some excellent clubs there. Great restaurants. And a rich history in jazz. Not as rich as Kansas City, of course, but . . ." Her eyes grew distant for a moment, then she shook her head. "I guess I can relate about being a little homesick."

"Not a lot of jazz clubs in Springfield?" he asked.

"Exactly zero, in fact," she said. "Apparently when DeCobray came in and rebuilt this town, the arts were not high on their list of priorities."

Stan wasn't a big arts person, but that did seem like an important thing for a town to have. "That's a shame."

"Well," she said, "we do what we can with what we're given, right?"

"What else can we do?" he agreed.

She turned to Julien. "I like this new friend of yours. He's got a good head on his shoulders."

Stan gave his friend a pained smile. If only she knew about his school discipline record.

"So what's this about a school club?" she asked Julien.

"Oh, uh, it's . . ."

Knowing his friend was terrible at lying, Stan jumped in. "It's a peer mentor program, so we do all kinds of stuff."

Ms. March looked impressed. "Peer mentoring, huh? I like the sound of that."

"Julien is basically a one-man tech support to the rest of the school."

"That's my baby!" She beamed.

"Mom . . ." said Julien.

Stan noticed that Julien's mom wasn't wearing a Lyre and decided a change of topic would be the safest bet.

"Ms. March, do you not have a Lyre device?"

"Oh, I got one all right," she said. "It's in my bedside table and that's where it will remain."

"My mom is not a tech person," said Julien.

"I swear, I have some sort of electrical thing in my body," Ms. March declared. "It all goes haywire when I try to use it."

Julien sighed. "I told you, that's not actually a thing, Mom. You just don't have any patience for it."

"So what if I don't?" she asked. "What do *I* need all that techno-stuff for? Give me a pen, some paper, and a piano, and I am happy."

Julien looked at Stan with a suffering expression. "My mom the tech-hater."

"I don't hate it," she said. "You love it, so I allow it in the house. But that doesn't mean I *like* it."

Given the fact that the Lyre devices could be used for such sinister purposes, Stan thought it was actually a good thing she wasn't using one.

Once they'd finished eating, Stan thanked Ms. March for dinner, said goodbye to Julien, and headed home. He felt a little pang of sadness, leaving the warm vibrant March house to return to his own house. He reasoned that since Mr. March was still at work, his mom probably was, too.

He was surprised, then, to see the lights on when he got home, and he found his mom sitting at the kitchen table, hands waving as she worked with her Lyre device. He felt a pang of discomfort seeing his mom wearing a device that he knew could cause such suffering. He doubted he could convince his mom to put hers in a drawer.

But he was also grateful that he hadn't come home to an empty house, after all.

"I hope you are not expecting me to make dinner for you when you come home so late," she said without looking.

He laughed. His mother might not be as warm and boisterous as Ms. March, but that was OK. She was his mom.

"No, I ate at a friend's house."

"Oh yes?" She turned to him, looking pleased. "Already making friends and settling in?"

"Uh, yeah, I guess."

"That is great. See? I told you this place would be good for us."

Stan wasn't sure he agreed that this place was good for them, but he really had made some good friends, so she wasn't completely wrong either.

"Yeah, I, uh, even joined an after-school club."

"What kind of club?"

"It's, like, peer mentor stuff. We help out other kids."

"Stanisław, that is such good news. I know you always want to help people, just like . . ."

Stan knew she wanted to say *like your father*, but she stopped short and just looked at him. He wasn't the only one who had been hurting since his father's death. His mom was all alone now. Not that he wanted a stepdad or anything. But he did feel bad for her.

"Anyway," his mother said, "you have found a way to help people that does not use your fists."

"Uh, yep." If only she knew . . .

Wait, should he try to tell her what was going on? If she was one of those people on the subway trains, she could be riding right past a mad scientist lab without knowing it. Maybe she could help them *do* something about it. Assuming she believed him.

"Say, Mom, did you know that there's a subway system in Springfield?"

"I would hardly call a single track a *system*, but yes, isn't it great? DeCobray offers it to all employees, which reduces the carbon footprint of Springfield." She sighed happily. "Such a great company. They give us so much."

"Yeah . . ." Just looking at her contented expression, he knew there was no way she'd believe him. Not without proof.

She smiled and touched his cheek. "I'm so glad we moved here, Stanisław. Aren't you?"

He noticed that she was still wearing her DeCobray employee badge. Except above her name wasn't the DeCobray logo. Instead, it was that same red cobra symbol. The sight of it chilled him.

"You bet, Mom." He forced a smile. "I'm thrilled to be here."

CHAPTER 16

A REAL INTIMIDATING TOWN

Scarlett had said they should act like nothing was wrong. Stan knew that wouldn't be easy, but he didn't expect to be tested before he'd even entered the school.

He froze when he saw Anastasia waiting at the entrance to Springfield Academy.

"Good morning, Stanisław," she said cheerfully, as though she hadn't kicked him in the chest and called him a fool two nights ago.

"Oh, hey, good morning, Baroness," he said, trying to hide his nervousness as he approached.

"I am sorry I wasn't able to perform my duties as your peer orientation counselor yesterday, but school assembly days are always so hectic."

"Sure, I understand." He looked around nervously. "Michel isn't with you?"

"No, it seems he was injured yesterday after school," she said without a lot of concern. "Some sort of chemical burn. I'm afraid he won't be coming to school for at least a few days."

"Oh . . ." Stan felt a stab of guilt. He still thought Michel was a terrible person, of course. And he certainly hadn't *meant* to spill that chemical. Even so, getting burned with acid wasn't something he'd wish on his worst enemy.

Anastasia frowned. "Stanisław, you don't seem to be wearing your Lyre device?"

"I was just about to put it in." He hastily shoved his hand in his pocket and awkwardly removed the earbuds from the shielding bag before taking them out and putting them in his ears. He figured if she saw the bag, it might draw more suspicion.

"You don't have to take your Lyre device off when you leave school," she said. "In fact, they are designed in such a way that you don't even need to take it off when you sleep."

"Oh yeah, they're very comfortable," he agreed. "I took it off to, uh, shower and just forgot to put it back in."

"Ah yes. Sadly they aren't completely waterproof yet."

"Real bummer," he lied.

"It's only a matter of time, of course," she said.

"What a relief."

She arched an eyebrow. "I assume you have been testing out the new Magica and Sciffy filters? Which do you prefer?"

"Um, I haven't actually had a chance to try them out yet. You know, I'm focusing on my school work, and the filters can be a little distracting."

"School work is important," she said. "But now that you are a student of Springfield Academy, you enjoy the many advantages of the Lyre device, and you are therefore expected to do your part to improve it. If you find filters too distracting during your classes, I suggest you test them out in the evenings."

"R-Right. Will do."

"Excellent." She paused, and her keen eyes drilled into his. "I look forward to hearing your *detailed* feedback."

He smiled weakly. "Sure thing, Baroness."

His eyes picked up on the student ID that his Lyre showed beside Anastasia. He'd gotten so used to the pop-ups that he barely even noticed them anymore. But now it occurred to him that all of the students had their hometowns listed. Except Anastasia. Why was that, he wondered.

"You had better get going, little Stanisław," she said. "You don't want to be late for your first class of the day."

"You bet."

He hurried inside, wondering just how much she knew, or at least suspected. He thought he'd played it fairly cool. But that didn't mean he was in the clear. In fact, it sort of felt like she was toying with him . . .

Or maybe that was just his imagination. He really hoped so.

The first bell rang, which meant he had only five minutes to get to his first class. Being late would draw even more attention, so he began walking faster down the hallway.

"Hey, Stan, you doing OK?"

A man stood in the open doorway of a faculty office. The faculty offices had frosted glass instead of the one-way mirrors, so people couldn't see inside. Stan didn't know this particular faculty member, but his Lyre device told him that it was Dr. Conrad Hauser, School Guidance Counselor. The guidance counselor had a blond crew cut and a rugged, square-jawed face like an old-fashioned Hollywood movie star. He also looked sincerely concerned about Stan's well-being. But after seeing what the principal of Springfield Academy was capable of, Stan wasn't about to trust *any* faculty at the school.

"Uh, yeah, I'm OK, Dr. Hauser. Thanks."

"Sorry, I know we haven't met yet." Hauser's brow furrowed. "Look, it can be hard to adjust to a new school and a new town all at once like this, especially in the middle of the year at an institution that's . . . well, a little unconventional. And I know it's not easy to open up, especially to an adult you don't know. But I'm always here if you need to talk to someone. Whatever we discuss will be confidential, strictly between you and me."

"Sure, Dr. Hauser. Thanks. That's good to know."

Yeah, right, thought Stan as he hurried on to his first class. *Not in a million years.*

A REAL HELPLESS TOWN

Faking like everything was totally fine for the entire day was even more stressful than Stan expected. He was constantly looking at the students that surrounded him, wondering how many of them were real. Sometimes he would even pretend to accidentally bump into someone just to make sure they were actually there.

But that was only part of the stress. He was also hyper-aware that he was wearing a device that could cause intense fear or anger at the tap of an invisible button.

How was that even possible? Anastasia had claimed that the devices were one-way only, but clearly she'd been lying. Regardless, his hand kept reaching up unconsciously to one of the buds, aching to yank it out. But he stopped himself each time. Julien had said they could probably tell when someone had their device off for too long during school hours. Of course, keeping it on posed its own dangers. Even if they didn't do something as obvious as making him go berserk in the middle of class, they might be tracking him and listening to him *constantly*. Before, he'd always thought "Who would bother with me?" Now there were people who might have a reason.

By the time he got to the clubhouse after school, he had a massive headache, and his jaw was sore from constantly clenching.

"Hey, Stan." Scarlett looked up from where she sat at a table with Zoro-me and Julien. "Are you OK?"

"Huh? Yeah." He dropped into an empty seat. "Sorry. I'm just really wound up about all this."

"Understandably," she said.

"Yeah, man," agreed Julien. "Last night I almost made

myself a tinfoil hat because I started worrying that the Lyre devices could affect us even if we weren't wearing them."

Stan stared at him, his anxiety ratcheting up even further. "*Can* they?"

"No," Julien said, then frowned. "Well, probably not." His frown deepened. "I mean in theory . . ." Then he shook his head. "Even if it were possible, as long as we keep them in the shield bags, that cuts the connection to their servers, rendering them more or less useless. I think."

"Speaking of which," said Scarlett. "We've all bagged our Lyres?"

They all nodded.

"Great. So has anyone managed to talk to the students we rescued yesterday?"

"Conner didn't come in today," said Julien. "Not even fake Conner."

Scarlett nodded. "That makes sense. Since they don't have the real Conner anymore, they can't risk him or the others showing up and people seeing doubles."

"But are they OK?" asked Stan.

"I called the hospital, but they don't give out information on patients," said Scarlett.

"Maybe we could check on them during visiting hours?" Julien asked.

"That's a good idea," said Scarlett. "I think they're still open for visitors a little while longer."

"Awesome," said Stan. "Julien and I can head over and check on Conner and any of the others who are around."

"Actually . . ." Scarlett turned to Julien. "I have an idea about addressing the larger Lyre device problem, but I need to pick your brain about some tech things."

"Oh, OK." Julien looked intrigued.

"But I still don't want you guys walking around by yourselves," Scarlett said firmly. "Zoro-me, can you go with Stan to the hospital?"

Zoro-me nodded.

They ended the meeting early, and Stan and Zoro-me walked though Springfield in silence. Of course, Zoro-me wasn't going to say anything, and he didn't seem bothered by the lack of conversation. Stan, on the other hand, was bothered by the silence but didn't know what to say that wouldn't sound like he was on the verge of freaking out, which, if he was being honest, he kind of was. His mind kept going back to that lab. Those kids. The screaming, fighting, laughter, and sobbing all at once. It really had been like something out of a nightmare. Yet Zartan, the *principal of his school*, had been watching it all like it was merely a science experiment. And Michel had been casually talking about where to put the bodies . . .

Stan shivered.

Zoro-me looked over at him.

"Sorry," said Stan. "I'm trying to be chill, but this town is like nothing I saw in Chicago or Kraków."

Zoro-me nodded.

Then Stan thought of something. "You know, as weird as Springfield is, it's also strange that a ninja family would move here. That can't be a coincidence."

Zoro-me shrugged.

"Tommy said something about the masters having a mission?"

Zoro-me tapped his lips.

"Yeah, OK, I guess it's a secret. That makes sense. Especially since you're ninjas. But can you at least tell me . . . your uncles are the 'masters' he was talking about, right?"

Zoro-me hesitated a moment, then nodded.

"They're really amazing, aren't they?"

An emphatic nod from Zoro-me.

"I know you've had a lot of bad stuff happen to you, but I guess getting adopted by them was a lucky thing."

"Lucky Snake-Eyes," said Zoro-me.

Stan honestly couldn't tell if his friend meant it as a joke or not, so he decided to let it pass without comment.

Springfield Hospital was, unsurprisingly, even more hi-tech looking than the school, with lots of smooth metallic curves and shining, LED-drenched glass. But it wasn't some big looming rectangle. It was all spread out, almost like a school campus. There were little topiaries and what looked like one of those Zen sand gardens.

They stared at the complex of structures for a few moments.

"Where do we even start?" asked Stan.

Zoro-me pointed to a sign that said ADMISSIONS.

"Good idea," said Stan. "They can probably tell us where Conner is."

The inside of the hospital looked bizarrely like the inside of the school, complete with glass walls.

"Does DeCobray only have one interior design?" Stan murmured.

Zoro-me's shoulder's bounced and he let out a single chuckle. Stan grinned. He was pretty sure that was the first time he'd ever heard his friend laugh.

They walked up to the reception desk, where a man was waving his hands in front of him. Stan's heart sank when he saw that, and when he checked, sure enough, the guy was wearing a Lyre device. He scanned the other employees, as well as the few people sitting in the waiting area, and they also had Lyre devices. It really was a citywide thing. But surely Zartan couldn't control the Lyre displays for everyone in the city. Right?

The man noticed Stan and Zoro-me standing there and swiped his hand to clear whatever he'd been looking at on his display.

"Can I help you gentlemen?"

"My friend Conner was admitted yesterday," said Stan. "I wanted to see how he's doing. Can you tell me where he is?"

"Sorry, we only give out room numbers to family."

"I see. Well, I, um, have some homework that he missed."

The man frowned. "Can't you send it to him with your Lyre?"

"Right, my Lyre . . ."

Stan desperately tried to think of something else to say, but Zoro-me touched his shoulder and jerked his head, like they should go.

"OK, uh, thanks anyway," Stan told the man.

"Sure thing," the man said, then went back to whatever he'd been doing on his device.

"Are we giving up?" Stan murmured as he and Zoro-me walked back toward the entrance.

Zoro-me shook his head. "He looked."

"Huh?"

Zoro-me tilted his head down a hallway. As they walked past it, he glanced back to make sure the man was preoccupied, then steered Stan around the corner.

"You saw him look this way when I asked about Conner?"

Zoro-me nodded.

"I didn't even notice," said Stan. "I guess that's ninjas for you. So, he's down this way, huh?"

The good thing about glass walls, Stan decided, was that it made finding someone's hospital room really easy. After only a few minutes, he spotted Conner. He was all bandaged up and looked pretty rough. Stan's heart sank even lower when he saw him swiping his hands around, a Lyre device in his ears. Stan didn't have high hopes for their conversation, but he went in anyway.

"Hey, Conner, how you feeling?" he asked cheerfully.

Conner looked at him, his brow furrowed. "Do I know you?"

Naturally he wouldn't remember meeting Stan at lunch, since that hadn't been the real Conner. But Stan had called him by name down in the lab.

"You don't remember me?" he asked carefully.

"Oh, sorry." Conner's expression got a little hazy. "Things are kind of a blur for me. I guess I got kidnapped or something? That's what the police said, anyway."

Should Stan tell Conner that he and Zoro-me helped rescue him? He kind of wanted to, but it probably wasn't wise. For one thing, Conner still had his Lyre in, so someone could be listening. Or Conner might tell Zartan who his rescuers had been, even innocently, and that would probably spell the end for them.

So instead he pretended ignorance. "Oh man, that's scary. Do they know how you got free?"

Conner shook his head. "No, they just found me and some other kids in front of the ER. Hard to believe, huh? Kidnappers right here in Springfield?"

"Mind-blowing," agreed Stan. "Well, I hope you feel better. Julien says hi."

"Oh, you know Julien? Cool. Tell him I hope I'll be well enough to make it to the next tournament so I can finally prove the superiority of Donkey Kong Junior."

"I'll let him know," promised Stan.

He and Zoro-me found the rest of the students, but they all said the same thing as Conner. Almost *exactly* the same thing. As if they had been coached to say it.

Stan groaned in frustration as they left the last boy's room. "That's it, then. At least they all seem fine physically. Let's go."

They left the hospital and started walking back through town. In the silence, Stan's mind was racing.

Had Zartan gotten to them? Or was the hospital staff in on it? They all had Lyres, so maybe Zartan *could* control every device in the city. Or maybe the hospital staff were also evil. Or at least some of them. How many adults besides their parents they could even trust?

A sick dread filled his stomach. What about his mother? She had a Lyre device, after all. Maybe they were doing things to her at work? No, she wouldn't let them hurt her. Unless she didn't know? But that didn't make sense. How would she not know that? Maybe they were making her do things to other people. *Hurting* others, and she didn't even know . . .

Suddenly it got really hard to breathe. Stan's heart pounded in his chest, and his hands didn't look right. They looked too big, like someone else's hands. And his feet. It was like he was walking on stilts. Was it the Lyre device? No, he wasn't wearing it. But what if it really could be affecting them even when they weren't wearing it. And what if the shielding bags didn't work as well as they thought? What if they were attacking his mind right now—

Zoro-me gripped his shoulders and forced him to stop.

"Breathe," he commanded. "Slowly."

Stan forced himself to take a deep breath, but it didn't help.

"Panic attack," said Zoro-me.

"I'm . . . having . . . a panic attack?" gasped Stan.

Zoro-me nodded.

Somehow, simply knowing he was having a panic attack and not getting his brain invaded helped a lot. His chest started to ease, and his pulse slowed back down. He continued to breathe deeply for a few minutes, then nodded.

"Thanks."

Zoro-me released his shoulders and stepped back.

Stan sighed. "Sorry. I guess I'm no good at this. It's like . . . Scarlett's a strategist. Julien is a hacker. You're, well, a *ninja*. But me? What am *I* good for? I wish I could contribute somehow. It's like . . ." He clutched at his chest, which still ached a little from his panic attack. "I have all this *stuff* inside me, you know? And I don't know what to *do* with it. I guess that's why I freaked out. Because I'm so frustrated and helpless, it feels like I might explode."

Zoro-me didn't respond. He probably didn't understand what Stan was talking about. After all, he was so ridiculously awesome that he probably *never* felt as helpless as Stan.

"Anyway," he said at last. "Sorry if I worried you. Let's go."

They continued on toward Stan's house. He assumed Zoro-me wanted to make sure he got home OK. But then at one intersection, Zoro-me stopped him and indicated they should turn right.

"My house is this way," he told his friend.

Zoro-me gestured for Stan to follow him.

Stan realized the dojo was in that direction.

"You want me to come back to the dojo with you?"

Zoro-me nodded.

"Are you sure your uncles aren't still mad?"

Zoro-me gestured again, this time impatiently.

"OK, OK. I'm coming."

Stan followed Zoro-me back to the dojo, wondering what they were going to do when they got there, or if Tommy would still want to beat him up.

Fortunately, there was no one else at the dojo. At least, not as far as Stan could tell. With ninjas, you never really knew for certain.

Once they'd taken off their shoes, Zoro-me had Stan stand in the middle of the tatami mat. Zoro-me stood beside him so they were facing the same direction, then he started punching the air in the same way over and over again.

Stan stared at him.

Zoro-me stopped and looked expectantly at him.

It took Stan a moment to understand. "You want *me* to do that now?"

Zoro-me nodded.

Stan tried to copy what he'd seen Zoro-me do, but almost immediately his friend shook his head, grabbed him by the wrist, yanked his arm further out, then smacked his shoulder.

"Ow, geez!" said Stan.

Zoro-me yanked and smacked again.

"I get it, I get it. Stretch my arm out more when I punch."

Zoro-me nodded and took a step back.

Stan tried again, but Zoro-me was immediately back in there, yanking and smacking him.

"Ichi No Zoro-me-sensei." Hādo appeared beside them,

his stern face even more disapproving than usual. "You are too easy on your pupil."

"Are you kidding me?" objected Stan. "He's slapping me all over the place!"

Hādo turned, and the old man's gaze weighed so heavily, Stan involuntarily took a step back.

"You would be wise to *never* contradict the Hard Master," said Hādo. "That is, if you truly want to learn the art of ninjutsu."

Stan stared at him for a moment. "Me? A *ninja*?"

Zoro-me nodded, then clutched his hand against his chest just like Stan had done earlier.

That's when Stan realized that his friend *did* understand what it felt like to be helpless and frustrated. Maybe this was what had helped Zoro-me get through that, and now he was passing it along to Stan.

He bowed awkwardly. "Thanks, Zoro-me."

Then he felt his feet swept out from under him, and he barely caught himself before getting a face full of tatami mat.

"That bow was terrible!" declared Hādo. "Try again!"

CHAPTER 18

>>>>>>> **A REAL ALTRUISTIC TOWN** >>>>>>>

Stan had to walk a little slower on his way to school the following morning. There was no place on his body that did not ache from his training. But at the same time, he felt so much better. It was like all the worry and stress had drained right out of his body.

Once he reached school, he steeled himself for another day of faking like everything was fine and wearing a potentially evil piece of technology in his ears. But he felt a little more confident that he could handle it now. He might not be moving at lightning speed or appearing out of nowhere like the Arashikage family any time soon, but at least he was *doing* something. And some day, eventually, he might even become a ninja.

Even better, Anastasia wasn't waiting for him at the front door, implying threats and demanding to know what he thought of the new filters.

On his way to his first class, he passed by the guidance office and saw that Dr. Hauser was once again standing in the doorway.

"Looking a little better today, Stan. Whatever you're doing, keep it up."

"Uh, thanks, Dr. Hauser. I will."

Stan hurried on, still really not at all sure about that guy.

At their club meeting, he grimly reported the conversations with Conner and the other students that they'd rescued.

"They don't remember *anything*?" asked Julien, looking crestfallen.

"I was afraid of that," said Scarlett. "It doesn't mean they won't remember later, but we can't just sit around and wait for it to happen."

"So what's the plan?" Stan asked eagerly.

She glanced at Julien. "We're still working out the logistics."

"It is a *lot*," he agreed. "So far no major showstoppers. But we're probably only going to get one shot at this, so we need to be absolutely sure it will work."

"I think we'll have it by the end of the weekend," said Scarlett. "In the meantime, you two should spend your time training."

"Oh . . . You knew that Zoro-me is training me now?" Stan felt embarrassed for some reason.

She looked amused. "Of course. In fact, I think it's perfect timing."

"For what?" Stan asked.

"To prepare for your infiltration mission."

"*Infiltration*?" asked Stan.

"That's what ninjas do best, isn't it? We know the Lyre devices require a server to function. We think they use a server room on school grounds. If we can shut that down, everyone's device goes dead."

"*Possibly*," chimed in Julien. "Still not sure about redundancies."

Scarlett nodded. "So Stan, you and Zoro-me will train for your infiltration, while Julien and I prepare the tools you'll need to make it happen. I think we should be good to go by Monday."

"Am I going to be ready for some actual ninja infiltration by next week?" Stan asked dubiously.

Zoro-me gave a firm nod.

"If you say so . . ."

After the meeting, Stan and Zoro-me walked to the dojo for another few hours of intensive training. Zoro-me started the session by drilling basic punches and kicks, making sure Stan's form was correct. He was getting the hang of that a little bit. There were lots of details about his own body positioning that he hadn't even thought about at first. But after getting smacked a bunch of times, he was much more aware of those things, and it was starting to become muscle memory.

But then they did an exercise where Stan and Zoro-me faced each other, their hands in front of them, palms pressed against the other person's. The goal was to push their opponent off-balance. It sounded easy.

It wasn't. When Stan tried to shove Zoro-me, his

friend anticipated the move and stepped back at the last second so Stan fell forward. Every single time. He tried to do it extra fast. He tried to take Zoro-me by surprise. It never worked. And if he tried to go on the defensive, Zoro-me invariably caught him off guard.

As he was picking himself up off the mat for probably the hundredth time, he noticed that Yawarakai was watching them.

"I really suck at this, don't I?"

The old man beamed with his usual kindergarten-teacher demeanor. "Of course you do. You are just a novice, after all. Ichi No Zoro-me-kun has been training since he was eight years old."

"But do you think I have a chance?" Stan asked plaintively. "Do I have, like, any natural ability at all?"

Yawarakai considered that a moment. "Natural ability? No, none to speak of."

Stan winced. Apparently, despite his name, the Soft Master could be pretty harsh.

"But," continued Yawarakai, "that is not the most important thing. In fact, natural ability can be a liability, because it does not encourage diligence and discipline.

Someone with a great deal of natural ability can quickly become complacent. Perhaps even arrogant."

"What *is* the most important thing, then?" asked Stan.

"Purpose," said Yawarakai.

"Purpose?" asked Stan. "I'm not sure I have that either."

"No?" Yawarakai's eyebrows rose. "Then what was it you were doing during all those fights at your last school in Chicago? Was it merely sport for you?"

"Of course not!" said Stan. "I don't enjoy fighting. But kids were getting picked on. What was I going to do—let it happen?"

Yawarakai nodded. "Is there a greater purpose than helping those in need?"

Stan felt something stir inside him. Pride, maybe? A new way of looking at things? In fact, it was the exact opposite of what those two cops had told him after his father's murder.

"It seems you already know the answer." Yawarakai turned and began walking toward the back rooms. "You'll stay for dinner, of course, Stan-kun."

"Oh, uh thanks, Sensei." Stan's eyes narrowed. "Wait,

how did *you* know I used to get into fights all the time at my old school?"

Yawarakai looked over his shoulder. "Did you really think we would let you befriend our treasured nephew without looking into your background? We *are* shinobi, after all."

"Oh." Stan wondered what would have happened if they hadn't liked what they found, then he decided he didn't want to know.

Zoro-me tapped him on the shoulder and gestured that they should continue training.

As they began once again, at least now Stan felt a little less despairing. He might not have talent, but he had purpose. That was probably why Yawarakai had spoken to him. When Stan thought about it, he was actually being taught by *three* ninjas, rather than just one. There might be a lot of terrible things going on in Springfield, but at least this one thing was pretty amazing.

A REAL CUTTING-EDGE TOWN

After his training session and dinner, Stan trudged home, exhausted but happy. Yawarakai was right. Helping people wasn't stupid. It was awesome.

"You seem cheerful," observed his mother when he arrived. "Another night at the dojo?"

"Yeah."

He plopped down on the couch. It had barely fit in their old apartment but now looked ridiculously small in their big new house. He wondered if his mom still planned to go furniture shopping that weekend, but before he got around to asking, she spoke first.

"I am really proud of you, Stanisław. Making friends, joining a school club, and now this new passion for martial arts. It is a great way to channel all that rowdy energy you have, my little Clash. I told you that Springfield would be good for us."

He smiled tiredly. "You did say that, Mom."

"Well, I will not rub it in anymore."

"Promise?"

"No," she admitted.

"I guess you like it here?" he asked tentatively. "You know, at work?"

She looked at him like he was crazy. "Is that a joke? I am working at the headquarters of the most advanced science and technology company in the world. No other employer could give us the level of funding and resources that DeCobray provides."

"Oh, yeah?" He realized this could be his chance to figure out what was really going on at DeCobray and just how much his mom knew. "So . . . what is it you do there, anyway?"

Her eyes narrowed. "After all these years, you are suddenly interested in what I do?"

He shrugged. "Just curious. Is it, like, top secret or something?"

"We do have to sign non-disclosure agreements," she said. "After all, we cannot have cutting-edge DeCobray technology leaking to the media before it is ready to be announced."

"Cutting-edge tech, huh? Even more than the Lyres?"

"Oh sure."

"Like what?"

She came over and sat down next to him. "Well, I am not supposed to say, but since you are finally interested, I will tell you a little. DeCobray is developing all kinds of interesting technologies. Gene therapy, advanced robotics, AI, neurological reframing—"

"Neuro-what?" Stan asked, maybe a little too sharply.

"That is the project I have been working on, actually. Did you know that nearly one in five Americans live with a mental illness?"

"No, I guess not."

She nodded. "It is true. And for decades, mental health

treatments have relied on medication that often has troubling side effects. The way the Lyre device works, it bypasses your eyes and ears, and communicates directly with the occipital and temporal lobes of your brain, which process sight and sound, respectively."

"Using brain wave entrainment and cranial electrical stimulation?" asked Stan, remembering what Anastasia had told him on the first day of school.

She looked pleased. "Correct. But did you know that the temporal lobe also affects your emotions? So imagine if we could use something like a Lyre device to treat depression, bipolar disorder, perhaps even schizophrenia, all without any side effects."

That sounded exactly like what Zartan had been doing to Stan's classmates, except not to help them.

"That would be pretty amazing . . ." he said carefully.

"It would indeed," she said, getting increasingly excited. "And we are so close! Very soon, I think DeCobray will be able to begin clinical trials. Can you imagine how many lives it would save, Stanisław?"

"I guess," said Stan. "But, like, if the Lyre can affect

our emotions, couldn't it also be used to mess up people who *didn't* have mental health issues?"

She frowned thoughtfully, as though she'd never considered the idea. "I suppose it could be reprogrammed for that purpose. But who would do such a terrible thing?"

"Yeah . . ." Memories of Connor and the other poor kids down in the mad science lab flashed through his head. "How could anyone be that evil?"

He wanted to tell his mother that this thing she was so proud of was being twisted by people like Zartan. But he hadn't seen her this excited about anything in a long time. Not since before his father died. And anyway, he had no proof, or even any witnesses. She'd never believe him.

CHAPTER 20

A REAL PRESENT TOWN

Stan thought his luck was holding when he didn't see Anastasia at the front door for the second day in a row. But the moment he entered the school, she was there.

"Ah, good. I see you remembered to put your Lyre device on after you showered this morning, Stanisław," she said by way of hello, which he thought was messed up on a *couple* of levels.

"Oh, yeah." He faked a smile as he tapped one of his earbuds. "You know I love this thing."

"I'm so glad to hear that," she said. "Because I have been thinking of recommending you for a special pilot program to test out new features."

He thought about the mood-controlling functions his mother had been talking about. "Oh, wow, that would be . . . neat."

"It would be a great privilege," she agreed. "But before we get into all that, what feedback do you have for me on the Magica and Sciffy filters?"

Of course, he hadn't tried out either of them. He was normally the sort of student who always did his homework, so he had no ready excuses to give her.

"Uh . . ."

"Hey, Stan!"

Relief flooded through Stan at the sound of Julien's voice.

"There you are, Julien!" He smiled as his friend entered the school. "I wanted to talk to you about that project we're working on."

"What a coincidence, me too!" said Julien. "Oh, hey, Baroness. How you been?"

Anastasia gave him a tight smile. "Just fine, Julien. And you?"

"Lovin' those new filters," Julien said enthusiastically. "I'm kind of partial to the Sciffy one. I got a soft spot for weird-looking alien dudes."

Stan was impressed at how cool Julien was acting. Maybe paranoia was making them all better liars. That was kind of a depressing thought.

"How fascinating," Anastasia said in a way that suggested she didn't find it interesting in the slightest. "But this is perfect timing, Julien. I was just telling Stanisław about our new pilot program. And since you're so passionate about technology, I thought—"

"That is a great idea, Baroness," Stan said with feigned enthusiasm. "Can't wait to talk to you about it more later. But we really do have to work out this project presentation before class starts."

Her temple twitched in annoyance. "Very well. Until next time, then."

"You bet!" Julien said, then the two hurried down the hall.

Once they were out of earshot, Stan murmured, "We really do need to talk."

"It's going to have to wait until we get to the club-house," said Julien.

Stan nodded. They were both wearing their Lyre devices, after all, and with Anastasia acting so suspicious, it was even more likely that someone was monitoring what they said.

Waiting until the end of the school day to deliver his new intel on the Lyre tech was tough, but Stan had learned some breathing techniques at the dojo that kept his anxiety from getting too out of control. Still, it was a huge relief when he could finally yank off his Lyre device and shove it into his shield bag, then hurry across the field to their clubhouse.

As fast as he got there, Scarlett and Zoro-me were still waiting for him. He had no idea how they both got there so quickly every day. Julien showed up shortly after.

"I think I know what Zartan was doing with those experiments," he told them.

He then recounted everything his mom had said the night before, watching their faces crease further and further with worry.

"Man, these Lyres are even more invasive than I thought," said Julien.

"Yeah, on my first day, Baroness claimed they didn't connect to your brain," said Stan. "I guess that was a big old lie."

"She *was* down there helping out Zartan and Michel," said Julien. "So she has to been in on all this stuff, right?"

"We should assume so," said Scarlett.

"But what is it for?" asked Stan. "Why make something that can make you super sad or super violent?"

"I can think of all kinds of reasons," she said. "They could use it subtly to influence people's opinions. Make them want to buy a certain product or vote for a certain politician. That kind of thing. Or they could use it more overtly and just turn a crowd of regular people into a homicidal mob."

Julien shivered. "Could you imagine something like that falling into the hands of a terrorist organization?"

"For all we know," said Scarlett, "this Cobra *is* a terrorist organization."

"We still don't even know if Cobra and DeCobray are the same thing, though," said Stan. "Having similar names isn't exactly proof."

"True," agreed Scarlett. "All we know for certain is that the principal of our school is somehow connected to both of them."

They stared at each other in silence for a moment as that reality settled in.

"So . . . what do we do?" Stan asked finally.

Scarlett chewed her lip, her brow furrowed. Finally she said, "I have to talk to someone about this."

"Who?" asked Stan.

"Sorry, I can't tell you. Yet. Please just trust me for now."

"I guess we've come this far," said Julien.

"Yeah, OK," said Stan. "But you will tell us eventually?"

She nodded. "Hopefully in a few days. In the meantime, Stan and Zoro-me, take the weekend to train as hard as you can."

"We will," promised Stan.

She nodded. "And Julien . . ."

"Yeah, I know what I need to do," he said.

She smiled gratefully. "Thanks, you guys. I'll check in with you all tomorrow, OK?"

After that, all Stan could really do was throw himself totally into his training.

It seemed that part of Zoro-me's training as a shinobi was to take on his own pupil. So while Zoro-me trained Stan, Hādo and Yawarakai trained Zoro-me on how to train. That was why they'd been so involved in Stan's lessons.

Tommy came by now and then to watch his progress. He didn't say much, but at least he didn't make fun of Stan's efforts. Scarlett showed up on Saturday as promised. She watched them train for a little while and joined them for Yawarakai's homemade dorayaki when they took a lunch break. After they ate, she and Tommy went off to a corner to talk quietly. Whatever they talked about, it seemed to make them both mad. They didn't shout or anything obvious like that. But Scarlett's face was almost as red as her hair when she stormed out after, and Tommy left a short time later with none of his usual swagger.

Stan wondered what Tommy did with his time. He was clearly aware of the bad things going on in Springfield, but he didn't seem to have any interest in helping the Joes make it right. Of course, more and more, Stan also wondered what Uncle Hādo, aka the Hard Master, and Uncle Yawarakai, aka the Soft Master, were really doing in Springfield. Especially since their dojo didn't seem to ever offer any actual martial arts classes to the public.

On Sunday, Scarlett came by again, which was a little embarrassing because she was there to witness just how terrible Stan was at the pushing "game."

"Terrible!" declared Hādo when Stan was shoved to the ground for the millionth time.

Stan sat up, his hip and hands throbbing with pain. The tatami mats offered some cushion, but not a lot. He drew his feet in, sighed, and put his head on his knees.

Scarlett cleared her throat. "With the greatest respect, Hādo-sensei, may I make a small request?"

He turned to her, a thick gray eyebrow raised. "Oh? Very well. Go ahead, Shana-chan. What would you ask?"

"Perhaps just a nudge in the right direction? As a favor to me?"

He frowned at her. "You should not get in the habit of babying him."

"I won't," she promised.

"Very well." He turned back to Stan. "You need to pay attention."

Stan knew better than to directly contradict the Hard Master, so instead he phrased it as a question. "I'm not paying attention?"

"You look toward the future."

"The future?" asked Stan. "I don't understand."

"You try to anticipate your sensei's actions."

"I shouldn't do that?"

Hādo shook his head. "Whether you try to look forward a day, or an hour, or five minutes, or two seconds, it is pointless. Are you a fortune-teller? How could you possibly know what he will do?"

"Well sure, but—"

Hādo's eyes hardened, and Stan stopped, realizing he was about to contradict him. He thought for a moment on how best to express his thoughts.

"How am I to avoid being pushed over if I can't anticipate his moves?"

Now Hādo nodded, looking a tiny bit pleased. "When you face your sensei, you continually ask yourself the wrong question. Do not ask 'what if.' Instead ask 'what *is*.'"

"What is . . ." Stan mulled that over. "So you mean—"

"Enough talk," snapped Hādo. "Begin again."

Stan and Zoro-me once again stood face-to-face, palms pressed against their opponent's.

What is . . .

Not what Zoro-me *might* do, but what he was doing in the present moment. Asking that question, over and over, each moment. What is he doing now? And now? And now?

It took Stan a surprising amount of focus to stop himself from guessing, anticipating, and assuming and only look at what was there. To see Zoro-me stand there and to think of nothing else. To see his foot tilt slightly.

Instinctively, he leapt back, and Zoro-me fell forward.

"Oh ho!" said Hādo, actually looking impressed. "You finally end the battle within yourself."

"Battle?" asked Stan as he helped Zoro-me back up.

"When you try to anticipate the future, you are at war with the present, creating anxiety and self-doubt. This conflicts with your desire to succeed, and so there is a great clash of wills within you."

Stan let out a small laugh. "A clash, huh? That's actually the nickname my dad gave me when I was little. Clash. Like the band."

"Until now, you have always tried to think ahead, fighting with your own better instincts," said Hādo. "But combat is a conversation, and your bodies are the voices. When someone speaks, you hear subtle inflections of tone that suggest their emotions and perhaps even intentions, do you not?"

"Sure," agreed Stan.

"You must learn to see subtle shifts in stance and posture for the body that will give you similar clues."

Stan stared at Hādo, then at Zoro-me, his eyes wide. "You know, I think I actually get it."

"Then you are beginning to wake up to the world around you," said the Hard Master.

"Congratulations, Clash," said Scarlett.

"Huh?" said Stan.

She shrugged. "You'll need a code name if we communicate on a mission. Might as well be one that you're familiar with."

"I guess yours is Scarlett." He turned to Zoro-me. "What's yours?"

Zoro-me shrugged. "Snake-Eyes."

"Of course it is," said Stan.

"What else would it be?" asked Scarlett.

Hādo chuckled quietly.

A REAL SURPRISE TOWN

Monday came much too quickly. As hard as it was training at the dojo, Stan felt like he would be happy to do it every day. Especially now that he'd made his first real breakthrough.

Maybe it was wishful thinking, but Stan felt like he was seeing everything from a slightly different angle as he walked to school the next morning. Hādo said he was starting to wake up to the world, and it actually kind of felt like that. Instead of stressing about all the bad things that might happen once he got to school, he was instead acutely aware of what was around him in that moment. The morning breeze, the rustle of leaves in the trees, the quiet hum of a car as it drove past. Maybe all that practice to be present in the moment during combat could be used in other ways. If nothing else, it made him appreciate his pleasant walk to school.

It also helped him spot Anastasia lurking just inside the door. He found a large upperclassman to keep between them and managed to slip past her without any fuss.

Another day of successfully avoiding getting roped into some sketchy "pilot program."

Each morning, Principal Zartan appeared on their Lyre devices to give the morning announcements. That morning, he wore a cream-colored suit with a crimson tie and pocket square. Then, after the usual sort of announcements, he surprised them by saying there would be another school assembly in a couple of days.

"Now, I know what you're thinking!" Zartan flashed his perfect, pearly white smile. "Principal Zartan, we just had an amazing school assembly with two great new filters! How could you possibly top that so soon? But trust me, this one is going to be *special*."

There was something about the way he said it that sent a chill down Stan's spine.

That afternoon, he expressed his worry at the clubhouse.

"He's planning something," he told his friends. "Something *bad*. I know it."

"Regardless," said Scarlett, "tonight we're going forward with our plan."

"Really?" Stan asked in surprise. "You mean we're ready to—"

"Sneak into Dr. Hauser's office?" she cut him off. "Absolutely."

He'd never heard of this plan, and was about to say as much, but then Zoro-me spoke:

"Yes."

Zoro-me never chimed in like that, especially when a simple nod would suffice. He only ever spoke when there was some purpose to it.

"That's right," said Scarlett. "As you all remember, we need to steal student records so we can see who else we can recruit for our club, and the most complete records are in the guidance counselor's office."

"Yes," Zoro-me said awkwardly once again.

It was like he was telling Stan to go along with it for some reason.

"Right," he said weakly. "*That* mission."

"Hold up—" began Julien, who clearly wasn't getting it.

"Yeah, hold up." Stan fixed his eyes on Julien. "We need to message our parents that we'll be coming home late tonight."

Julien still looked confused, but at least he didn't object any further.

"Of course," said Scarlett. "In fact, everyone should head home for now, and we'll meet tonight in front of the school at eight."

"Yes," Zoro-me said once more.

"Great." Stan gave Julien another meaningful look. "Let's head home, then."

"Right . . ."

The two friends left school and walked in silence for about a block until finally Julien burst out.

"OK, what was that all about?"

"No idea," admitted Stan. "But Zoro-me definitely wanted us to go along with it."

"This was not the plan," insisted Julien. "I know the plan. Or at least I thought I did . . ."

"I'm sure Scarlett has a good reason," Stan assured him. "She's been right so far, hasn't she?"

"Yeah, but I'm not, like, an action dude, and breaking into faculty offices is definitely not my thing."

"Mine either," said Stan. "But she's been looking out for me since my first day here. So I have to go with her on this one."

Julien sighed. "I hope you know what you're doing. *All* y'all."

Stan never came home this early and he didn't know what to do with himself once he got there. The house remained ridiculously empty, because they still hadn't gone furniture shopping. At least it gave him ample space to practice his ninjutsu.

He was just getting ready to leave when his mom got home.

"Are you going to the dojo at this hour?" she asked.

"No, it's a thing with my after-school club," he said.

"OK, but it *is* a school night, so don't be out too late."

"I won't," he said, unsure if he was lying or not. After all, he didn't actually know what Scarlett had planned.

When he got to the school, the bright, modern building seemed somehow more sinister than it did during the day. The glass was all dark and the chrome glinted ominously in the moonlight. Scarlett and Zoro-me were already waiting, and Julien showed up soon after.

"Sorry, my parents were not big on me being out this late, so I had to sneak out."

"Really?" Stan asked in surprise.

"What, your mom was cool with it?" Julien looked envious.

Stan thought about the many times he had been allowed to roam the streets at night back in Chicago. He wasn't sure if it was just his mom, or a general Slavic thing, but she always complained that American parents hovered too much. "Let's just say she's encouraged independence from an early age."

"Now that we're all here, let's get going," Scarlett said briskly. "Zoro-me, if you'll do the honors."

Zoro-me somehow had a key, and he simply unlocked the front door and they all walked into the school. Stan wasn't really sure if it counted as "sneaking." But with all four of them there, it wasn't like stealth was an option. Still, were they really going to break into Hauser's office? For student records? There had never been any talk about recruiting new people at any of their club meetings.

When they reached the door to the guidance office, Scarlett looked at Zoro-me for a moment, then said, "Ready?"

He nodded and took out what looked like lockpicks, then knelt down in front of the office door.

"Well, well, well, what do we have here?"

Anastasia's voice boomed through the hallway. The lights blinked on, and Stan's heart sank when he saw not only the Baroness but Principal Zartan as well.

"What is the meaning of this?" demanded Zartan, his usual polished voice taking on an edge.

"It is as I told you, Principal," purred Anastasia. "This 'Average Joes' club *claims* to be a peer support group, but in truth they are nothing but troublemakers. Who knows what mischief they had planned by breaking into the guidance counselor's office."

Stan thought they were doomed for sure, but when he looked over at Scarlett, she didn't even look surprised. Instead, she simply lifted her hand and knocked on the door.

It opened immediately, and Dr. Hauser stood there, smiling his square-jawed Hollywood smile.

"Whoa, what's all the commotion out here?" he asked.

Zartan looked a little less confident now. "Oh, er, Dr. Hauser. I'm sorry to say that I just caught these students trying to break into your office."

Hauser gave a hearty chuckle. "Oh, no, sorry for the confusion, Principal. This is all a big misunderstanding. You see, Shana here was telling me that she was worried about the security of my office, since it contained such sensitive student information. I told her I wasn't convinced her concerns were warranted, so I challenged her and her club to try to break in and prove me wrong."

They all stared at him, even Zartan. It was a pretty far-fetched explanation, after all. The only ones who didn't seem surprised by it were Scarlett and Zoro-me.

"You . . ." Anastasia glared at Scarlett with pure hatred. Scarlett smiled blandly back at her.

"Dr. Hauser," Zartan said through clenched teeth. "You are *sure* that is the case?"

"You bet," Hauser said.

It hung there between them a moment, then Zartan sighed. "Very well. My mistake." His expression hardened as he turned on Anastasia. "And *you*, the next time you try to drag me into your petty student squabbles, you better think again, or it's a month of detention!"

She flinched and mumbled, "Yes, Principal."

"Get out of here!" he snapped, and she fled.

Zartan straightened his tie and looked back at Hauser, now smiling like it was a morning announcement. "Sorry about this, Dr. Hauser. Good night."

"Good night, Principal Zartan," said Hauser.

Once Zartan was gone, Hauser turned to Scarlett. "Wasn't *that* interesting."

She let out an explosive breath of relief. "It was *some-thing* anyway."

Hauser turned to the rest of them. "Why don't you kids come into my office for a minute."

Once they were all inside, Hauser closed the door, then walked over to his desk and picked up a little plastic rectangle with a single button. Compared to all the fancy DeCobray tech, it looked pitifully homemade.

He pressed the button on the rectangle, then turned to them.

"OK, that should give us a few minutes of privacy."

"What a minute . . ." Julien squinted at the rectangle. "That's like an old-school Wi-Fi scrambler, isn't it?"

Hauser nodded. "Made it myself. It'll disrupt the video feed for any wireless cameras that might have been planted in my office. Can't be too careful around here. Now, I'm sure you kids have a lot of questions."

"Uh, yeah," said Stan.

"Sorry for the mystery," Scarlett said. "This morning I found evidence that someone had been in the clubhouse over the weekend. Zoro-me and I searched everywhere and we couldn't find any cameras, but I was still worried that it had been compromised."

"So this was a test?" asked Stan.

"And clearly, I was right."

"OK, but where does *this* dude fit in?" Julien jerked his thumb at Hauser.

Scarlett looked expectantly at the guidance counselor.

He rubbed the back of his crew cut thoughtfully for a moment. "Scarlett assures me that you can be trusted, and right now I'm pretty desperate, so I'm going to have to take her word for it. You see, I'm part of a loose underground network of people that has been tracking DeCobray, or rather *Cobra*, for years now. Because of my credentials and background, I was able to get a job working here, but really I'm here to figure out what the heck Cobra is plotting. Although honestly, after more than a year, I didn't have much to show for it. Not until Shana and I started working together."

"I picked up on this underground group a little while back," said Scarlett, "and when Dr. Hauser and I realized we were working toward the same goal, we started sharing intel."

"*This* is the guy you were going to talk to that you couldn't tell us about," said Stan.

She nodded.

"Who is this underground network?" asked Julien. "What are we talking about here? Spies and dissidents? Black ops stuff?"

Hauser shook his head. "It's mostly folks who have been harmed by Cobra in some way. But we're all just normal people. Nobody special."

Stan grinned. "Just some average Joes, huh?"

Hauser laughed. "Sure."

"So Cobra is real . . ." said Julien.

"It is," said Hauser.

"And they're connected to DeCobray?"

"Somehow," said Hauser. "Although we still don't know a lot of specifics. Are they the same company? Partners? We just don't know yet."

"And my dad, and Stan's mom, work for these people. They just don't know it."

"Most DeCobray employees probably don't," said Hauser. "Otherwise there would have been a leak long ago. Because Cobra has been at this for years, and there has never been a shred of evidence to prove their crimes."

"Who's running it all?" Stan asked. "Who's behind Cobra? Is it Mr. DeCobray?"

"We don't know," said Hauser. "If it *is* Mr. DeCobray, he's putting on a really good act."

"Yeah, I've seen that dude's product launch presentations," said Julien. "There is nothing about him that even hints at 'evil mastermind.'"

"More likely, it's someone behind the scenes," said Hauser. "Although who that might be, we have no idea."

"We'll just have to find out," said Scarlett.

Hauser frowned at her. "Not *we*. You and I had this discussion. You and your friends were supposed to gather intel, nothing more. *No* direct confrontation. That was our deal."

She winced. "I know, I know. But if we hadn't pulled those kids out, Michel would have been tossing their corpses into the lake by the end of the night. What did you expect me to do?"

"Honestly, I probably would have done the same in your shoes," admitted Hauser. "But no more of that.

From now on, you kids stay clear and let me handle the rest. *Understood?*"

"Of course," said Scarlett.

"Good," said Hauser. "It's late. You all should go home."

They said good night to Hauser and filed silently out of the office.

Once they were outside the school, Stan cleared his throat. "So, uh, Scarlett . . . are we really just going to let Hauser handle the rest?"

"Of course not," she replied. "Like you said earlier, Zartan is probably planning something bad for the school assembly, which is in two days. I respect Dr. Hauser, of course, but we don't have time to wait around for adults to discuss things. Especially when we already have a plan ready to go. Isn't that right, Julien?"

He grinned. "I was about to say, ain't no way I gave up my entire weekend for nothing."

A REAL HIGH-WIRE TOWN

The following afternoon, Stan and the other Joes met at the dojo after school because it might be the only place left in town where Cobra wasn't listening.

"OK, here is my baby." Julien held up a tiny USB drive. "All you have to do is plug it into one of the Lyre servers, and it will do the rest."

"Of course, getting to the servers won't be easy," said Scarlett. "But I've figured out a way into the school that avoids all cameras except the one covering the server room itself, and we know exactly where that one is. With a little bit of . . . *borrowed* equipment . . ." She glanced around the room nervously. Neither Tommy nor the masters were at the dojo right then. As far as they knew. "The two of you should be able get to the server room and bypass that one camera long enough to get in there, do what you need to do, and get out."

Stan took the USB stick from Julien and looked curiously at it. "So what does it do? Shut down all the Lyres?"

"No, Scarlett and I decided that was too risky," said Julien. "If Cobra has any kind of redundancy—which hello, they're a big fancy tech company, they better— then as soon as we took the servers offline, the Lyres would probably just switch to using another server location. Maybe not as blazingly fast, but still fully functional."

"Plus, we'd tip our hand to Cobra," said Scarlett.

"So instead," said Julien, "I've created my own 'update' to the device software. Once it installs on the Lyres, it will force a reboot, and when the devices come back online, everything will still work the same *except* Zartan won't be able to take control of them anymore."

"No more secret filters or emotional manipulations?" asked Stan.

"Exactly," said Scarlett.

"There is one problem, though," said Julien. "Updates can only be pushed when the students are within close range of the servers. And the only way to make sure everyone gets the update is if they all get it at once. That's why Zartan always pushes out new filters during school assemblies."

"So we won't be able to install *our* update until the school assembly tomorrow morning," said Stan.

"Right around the time that Zartan is doing whatever *he* plans to do," said Scarlett.

"What if they both happen at the same time?" asked Stan.

Scarlett and Julien looked at each other.

"We have no idea," said Julien.

Once the sun began to set, they picked up their bag of "borrowed" equipment and headed over to the school. When they reached school grounds, they skirted the edge until they reached the wooded area in back. Then they located the specific tree that Scarlett and Zoro-me had scouted out earlier. This tree was the only one tall enough and close enough to the school to accommodate the plan.

Because the only way to avoid most of the cameras, it turned out, was by going in through the roof.

Once it was completely dark, Stan and Zoro-me climbed to the very top of the trunk, where it was thin, and swayed precariously with every movement. The first time it dipped to the side, Stan ordinarily would have panicked, but once again his ninja breathing techniques came in handy.

The two of them got into position, then Zoro-me fired the air-compressed grappling hook he'd "borrowed" from the Hard Master's stash of grown-up ninja gear. They were probably going to get in trouble for all the "borrowing," but they would worry about that later.

Right now, the bigger concern was climbing hand over hand on a rope that stretched one hundred feet from the tree to the top of the school building over a forty-foot drop. Scarlett had done some calculations and said that, statistically speaking, if they fell from that height, they'd have about a fifty percent chance of survival. Meaning they'd be lucky if all they did was break both their legs.

But height wasn't the only concern. A hundred feet was a long way across a rope. They both wore gloves, of course, but while Zoro-me's hands were incredibly calloused, Stan's weren't. And while Zoro-me could split cinder blocks with his hands, Stan hadn't even managed a wooden plank yet. Would he make it across before his hands tired out?

They weren't sure the rope could hold two people at once, so Zoro-me went first. He made it look so easy, smoothly swinging hand over hand along the rope. It took him only a couple of minutes to reach the rooftop. Once he was there, he made sure the grapple was secure, because Stan would probably not be doing it nearly as smoothly.

He started out pretty good. He had some nice initial momentum and moved almost as smoothly as Zoro-me had. He kept his eyes fixed on the rooftop and powered through until he reached the middle.

Then the tree began to sag, which made the rope dip down in the center, which in turn meant a difficult, uphill climb for the second half. He moved more slowly, and that gave him more time to notice just how high up he was.

His stomach lurched as he became aware of how much empty space was under his feet. The wind started to pick up, and with the new slack in the rope he began to sway from side to side. That tired him out more quickly, and his hands started to cramp up. Could he really do this after just a few days of training? Who was he kidding? But it was too late to go back. Whichever way he went, his arms would give out before he reached the end. He was basically already dead or crippled.

But he saw Zoro-me waiting for him on the roof, not seeming even a little worried. In fact, when he noticed that Stan was looking at him, he waved. Just a casual, everyday wave, like he was waiting for him across the street rather than across a terrifying chasm.

"Heh," said Stan.

For some reason, that calmed him down and allowed him to remember his training. He'd let the fear take over, and it had almost beaten him. He'd starting asking *what if?* again. But he didn't have the time or energy to waste on that. He just put one hand in front of the other. His fingers throbbed and his shoulders ached, but he gritted his teeth and kept going until finally Zoro-me was helping him up onto the roof.

Once he was standing, Zoro-me patted him on the back.

"Yeah, sure," said Stan, still breathing hard. "No problem."

Zoro-me nodded, then motioned for him to follow along the metal rooftop. They stopped at the far end and began unpacking the climbing gear they'd brought. Some of it was Scarlett's, but most of it was once again from the Hard Master's ninja gear stash, including the huge magnets that they would use as anchors for the repelling rope.

Stan was still a little fuzzy on a lot of the knots, pulleys, and hitches that went into climbing gear, so he let Zoro-me set it all up. Once they were done, Zoro-me handed him the harness.

"You sure I should be the one going down first?" he asked. "I mean, you're the actual ninja."

Zoro-me pointed to the rope anchor system, then lifted Stan's arm and made it flap like a limp noodle.

"Yeah, I guess my arms are probably too tired to lower myself down," he admitted.

So Stan climbed into the harness and buckled it on while Zoro-me positioned himself with the ropes. Once they were both ready, Stan stepped over to the edge of the building and looked down.

That was a mistake.

He thought that maybe after his rope climb, he'd be able to handle it better, but nope. The dread shot up into his stomach so fast and hard he thought he might throw up. Now he was grateful that Scarlett had convinced him not to eat dinner before they started.

It took him a few moments of breathing exercises to get his heart rate back down. Then he turned and began climbing down the side of the building while Zoro-me held on to the rope with the anchor system. Once Stan was over the side, he let go and Zoro-me slowly lowered him down to the window.

They'd chosen this particular window because it was one of the bathroom windows, and no matter how evil Cobra was, even they weren't going to put cameras in a kids' bathroom.

Julien had broken the lock on the bathroom window that afternoon to make sure it was accessible. It was pretty narrow, however, even for Stan. He had to hold his breath, and he definitely lost some skin as he forced himself through.

Once he was in the bathroom, he unclipped the rope from his harness and attached it to one of the thick metal pipes. Then he gave it two sharp tugs.

A few moments later, Zoro-me silently joined him, making it look much easier than Stan felt it was.

From there, the two friends snuck through the school, following Scarlett's careful instructions on avoiding the cameras. It was not the most direct route to the server room, but it got them there eventually.

They paused just before turning the corner, and Zoro-me took out a small scrambler, similar to the one Hauser had used. They could activate it to temporarily stop the camera from communicating with the network. Long enough for one of them to slip in, plug Julien's USB drive into one of the servers, and get out. The range on the scrambler was small, so the person holding it would have to stay near the camera.

Stan had assumed he would be the one to stay behind, but when he held out his hand, Zoro-me shook his head.

Me? mouthed Stan.

Zoro-me nodded.

This didn't really seem the time to let the newbie do the actual infiltration. But he wasn't about to argue with his sensei in the middle of a mission.

Zoro-me held up his hand, the other holding the scrambler. Then he pressed the button and dropped his hand. Stan had no way of knowing if the camera was working or not. He just had to trust that his friends were all doing their part.

He stepped around the corner and walked swiftly but carefully to the door. There was a security keypad, but somehow Scarlett had managed to get the code this time, so Stan didn't have to wriggle through any ducts. Instead, he quickly typed the code and held his breath.

A moment later, the pad turned green, and he yanked open the door.

It was very cold inside. Julien had warned him it would be intensely air-conditioned. Something to do with the servers kicking off tons of heat. When he first entered, he could see his breath.

Before him were rows upon rows of server racks. The way Julien had explained it to him, servers were basically just computers without monitors or peripherals. The electronic version of brains without bodies. It looked like there were hundreds of them in the room, if not thousands. The closer he got, the warmer the air felt. By the time he was close enough to touch them, it no longer felt cold at all.

They really did look like rows of computer PCs set in metal bookcases, each neatly on a rack, with thick braids of cables coiling up the side. They blinked and hummed quietly. And that was it.

To think, so much in the world was controlled by things like this . . .

Scarlett had told them to plug the USB stick into a server near the back, so it wouldn't be easy to spot. Stan had asked why they didn't just take it out right away, and Julien had explained that if didn't stay in until the update was deployed, someone with system administrator access could overwrite the install command remotely.

This at least forced them to physically go to the actual server room, locate the USB drive, and yank it out, all before tomorrow morning.

Stan threaded his way down the narrow aisle, careful not to bump into any of the cabling, until he came to the second-to-last column. He quickly located a USB port and slid Julien's masterpiece into it.

No alarms, no nothing besides a faint flickering light on the USB drive as it delivered its payload.

Stan let out an audible sigh. That was it. He'd done it. Mission accomplished.

Then he heard the hiss of steel and felt a knife at his throat.

CHAPTER 23

>>>>>>>>>>>> **A REAL ESCAPE TOWN** >>>>>>>>>>>>

"What are you doing here, eighth grader?"

It was Tommy's voice. Stan couldn't decide whether to be relieved or terrified.

"W-We're preventing Zartan from being able to manipulate people's Lyre devices. They'll finally be able to see the truth."

"Waste of time." But at least he removed the knife from Stan's throat.

When Stan turned around, he saw that instead of his

usual white hoodie, Tommy was decked out in the full yoroi, or ninja armor, including a cowl that covered most of his face. Although, for some bizarre reason, it was still white, which did not seem to Stan like a great way to hide in the shadows.

"How is it a waste of time?" he demanded.

"Most people don't actually want to see the truth," said Tommy. "In fact, they prefer all those distracting, fanciful filters because it helps them escape their dull and empty lives."

"Even if that's true," said Stan, "at least now they'll have the choice."

"As usual, Scarlett's sentimental idealism clouds her thinking. You shouldn't be wasting your energy on such trivial concerns."

"Zartan is planning to mess with the reality of every student in the school at tomorrow's assembly. That's not trivial."

He shrugged. "Only the weak will be harmed. And who cares about them?"

Stan's lip curled up. "*I* care."

"You're as bad as my brother, then."

"Good," Stan said defiantly.

"Where is he, anyway?"

"He's in the hallway keeping the camera scrambled."

"At least you weren't deluded enough to think you could do this on your own. You better be grateful that he's expending so much effort on you."

"I am."

Tommy turned to go but then stopped and looked back at Stan.

"Tell your sensei he needs to punish you for letting down your guard while you were still on mission."

Stan wanted to ask Tommy what *he* was doing sneaking around the school at night, but the white-clad ninja was already gone. How had he even gotten *in*?

Well, Stan didn't have time to worry about that now. Left on too long, the scrambler would draw its own kind of attention. So he hurried back along the aisle to the door, down the hall, and around the corner to where Zoro-me waited.

Stan considered telling Zoro-me about his brother, but he decided that would have to wait. Instead, he just gave a thumbs-up, and then they hurried back the circuitous route that Scarlett had given them to the bathroom.

Zoro-me went first, clambering nimbly up the rope without any harness. Then Stan clipped the rope to the harness and squeezed back out the window. His hands and arms had recovered somewhat, so he didn't need to completely depend on Zoro-me to pull him up to the roof, but it was still a comfort to know he wouldn't fall.

Once he was back on the roof, he said, "I ran into your brother."

Zoro-me nodded, not looking surprised for some reason. Then he gestured to the rope anchor system.

"Yeah, let's get out of here."

They unlatched everything and packed it up. Then they hurried back to their tightrope. Zoro-me added some slack to the line, then texted Scarlett. After a few minutes, the far end of the line dropped lower, so it was basically a zip line back to the trees. That was easily Stan's favorite part.

Scarlett and Julien were waiting for them at the base of the tree.

"Well?" Julien asked eagerly. "How'd it go?"

"We did it," said Stan.

"Did anyone see you?" asked Scarlett.

"Sort of," admitted Stan. "Tommy was there, decked out in full-on ninja gear."

"Ugh, that jerk," said Scarlett. "I'll bet he was there just to make fun of you."

"Seemed like it," said Stan. "How did he even get in?"

"I have no idea," admitted Scarlett. "He has some kind of secret access, and I asked him to tell me what it was. I *begged* him. But the only thing he was willing to give me was the code for the door."

Stan recalled the argument between Scarlett and Tommy at the dojo on Saturday and suspected that's what it had been about.

"Why does he need his own secret way into the school?" Julien asked. "Like, what does that dude even do, besides be a jerk?"

Scarlett glanced at Zoro-me. Then she said, "The Arashikages have their own goals here in Springfield. Fortunately for us, those goals don't necessarily conflict with our own, so the smartest thing we can do is stay out of their way."

"Fine by me," said Julien. "That Hādo guy is terrifying." He met Zoro-me's eyes. "No offense, man."

"We do *not* want them for enemies," agreed Scarlett. "Now, let's all go home and get some sleep. Tomorrow's going to be very exciting."

CHAPTER 24

>>>>>>>>> **A REAL PROBLEM TOWN** >>>>>>>>

"How exciting," said the Cobra Commander as he sat at his bank of monitors and watched the four teenagers hurry out of the woods and back toward their sad little domiciles.

There was a polite knock at the door.

"Come in," the Commander said.

"Commander, sir!" The Cobra soldier entered and saluted sharply. "TeleViper Squad requests permission to send in a team to clean the servers at Springfield Academy immediately!"

"Now, why would we do a thing like that?" the Commander asked.

"W-Why, sir?" The soldier looked baffled. "Because this intrusion might interfere with Zartan's beta test of the new Lyre functionality?"

"It might," conceded the Commander. "But that is not a priority project. And I am *very* interested to see where this goes. No, tell TeleViper Squad to stop their hand-wringing and simply firewall the Academy servers so they don't infect the rest of the network."

"Yes sir."

"Oh, but make sure our dear golden boy is back on his feet. Give him some toys—nothing too egregious, although a *little* fun is OK—and send him on his way. I'd hate to think this precocious quartet might get the mistaken idea that we don't care about their charming exploits."

"Right away, sir!" The soldier saluted again, then left.

The Commander continued to gaze at the tree line

where the four teenagers had recently been scheming their little schemes.

Then he saw a momentary flicker of white.

"Hmm." He tapped his fingertips together. "Now *that* is a problem."

A REAL MOB TOWN

The previous night, Scarlett had told Stan and the others, "We have no idea what we're getting into tomorrow. We better stick together for the assembly."

So they met up a block away from the school, looking tense and tired. They'd been out pretty late, and even Stan had had to do some fast-talking to appease his mother.

"We're going to have to wear our Lyres so we don't draw attention to ourselves," said Scarlett.

"Which means that until Julien's update installs, we

might be as vulnerable as everyone else to whatever Zartan has planned," said Stan.

She nodded.

"The assembly is supposed to start at eight-thirty," said Julien. "I set the update to deploy at eight-thirty-five in case there are any latecomers."

"Good idea," said Scarlett.

"Yeah, how much damage can Zartan cause in five minutes?" asked Stan.

Julien gave him a horrified look. "Why did you have to go and jinx it like that?"

"Whatever he has in store," said Scarlett, "we'll be ready."

Zoro-me nodded.

They walked the last block to school as a group. Stan realized that if they were in a movie, this would be that slo-mo moment where everyone was walking in a line, looking cool and heroic. Sadly, they were not movie heroes. They were just four average Joe teenagers trying to do the right thing.

One good thing: Stan noted that Anastasia wasn't lurking at the door for him that morning.

Or was that a bad thing?

Either way, they headed down the hallways of see-through classrooms, surrounded by boisterous teenagers. The other students were talking excitedly to each other, speculating on what new feature their Lyres were about to get. Support for third-party apps like games and streaming services was the most hoped for feature, although video chat was also high on the wish list.

The four Joes entered the auditorium and sat together in the last row by the exit. Just in case.

Stan kept glancing at the time in the upper corner of his Lyre display. Eight twenty-five. Ten minutes until the update.

"What if it doesn't work?" muttered Julien. "What if I messed up the coding?"

"You didn't," Scarlett assured him.

"What if someone already pulled the drive out and overwrote the update?" he asked.

"They only had about a ten-hour window to do that," she pointed out. "It's unlikely they would even notice it was there in that time."

Julien nodded but still looked worried. Stan couldn't

blame him. The room was packed with hundreds of students, and their continued well-being might be riding on his programming skills.

At exactly eight-thirty, the lights in the auditorium dimmed.

"I was kind of hoping he'd start a few minutes late . . ." muttered Julien.

Just like last time, Zartan appeared alone on the stage, looking as dapper as ever. This time he was dressed in a mint-green suit with a purple tie and pocket square.

"Good morning, students of Springfield Academy!"

The students cheered like they had the time before.

"Wow, do I have something amazing planned for you this morning," he said. "A really special treat!"

Excited whispers rippled through the crowds.

8:31 A.M.

"For some time now, we've been testing out the academic and productivity features of the Lyre," continued Zartan, his expression thoughtful. Contemplative almost. "How to utilize them for school and work, right? But you know, they can be used for so much more."

8:32 A.M.

Stan found himself checking the clock constantly, wondering what would happen in the next few minutes. Thinking *what if* . . .

No wait. He should be asking what *is*.

"DeCobray isn't just concerned about profits and productivity," Zartan was saying. "They want to capture the hearts and minds of people as well. After all, it's not called the Lyre AR device, it's the *XR*, because it extends beyond what we can see and hear, reaching into what we can *feel*."

Stan looked more carefully at Zartan. That's when he noticed the principal wasn't casting any shadow.

8:33 A.M.

He yanked off his Lyre. The stage was empty.

"Zartan's not even *here*," he hissed to his friends.

All three pulled off their Lyres as well.

Scarlett's eyes widened. "This is bad . . ."

"And of course," Zartan's voice boomed over the speaker system, "the most efficient way to capture hearts and minds is by using our revolutionary advancements in brain wave entrainment and cranial electrical stimulation!"

Stan felt a chill at hearing those words. He didn't need to anticipate. He *knew* what would happen next.

8:34 A.M.

Suddenly, all the other students stood up in their seats, faces creased with a mindless fury, their bodies tense and shaking, as if barely holding themselves back from going wild.

"Oh dear," Zartan's voice said. "You four have already taken off your Lyres. Well, I guess you'll have to be on the *receiving* end of this test."

Hundreds of angry faces turned toward Stan and his friends.

"Run," said Scarlett.

They scrambled out of their seats, and Zoro-me slammed his shoulder into the emergency exit door. But it wouldn't budge.

"You didn't think it would be that easy to escape, did you?" asked the disembodied voice of their principal. "Not this time, and not down in the lab either. You thought I couldn't work out who you were? And poor Michel! You really did a number on him."

8:35 A.M.

Stan and his friends pressed their backs against the door as their fellow students climbed over seats, moving in a slow but steady wave toward them, faces twisted with rage.

"Uh . . . Julien?" asked Stan.

"It's gonna take a minute to install, isn't it?" his friend snapped testily.

Zartan's voice continued, "I was pondering a tragic accident cover story for your deaths. But that might bring too much media attention to my little science experiment. And why bother, when I can simply make people think you're still here?"

The rage mob of students drew closer, hands twitching like they hungered to cause hurt. Stan, Scarlett, and Zoro-me shifted into a fighting stance. They didn't want to hurt their fellow students, but it didn't look like they had much choice. Not that Stan could fend off that many people at once. But he wouldn't go down without a fight.

"Anyway," said Zartan, "thank you for your noble sacrifice in the name of science. It will be remembered. Well, by me, anyway. Everyone else won't even notice you're gone. Now, my dear students of Springfield Academy . . . *Kill them!*"

A terrifying roar went up as the students surged forward.

Stan steeled himself.

Then the mob froze, and after a moment, their faces went slack.

"Finally, the reboot," sighed Julien.

A moment later, the students all seemed to come back

to themselves at once. They looked around, confused, asking each other what happened.

Stan clapped Julien on the back. "You did it."

Julien looked relieved enough to fall over. "Yeah. I guess I did . . ."

"We never doubted you," said Scarlett.

Zartan's voice came back on over the speakers, seething with barely suppressed wrath. "Sorry, students. We've had some sort of glitch in the update. It seems we're going to have to . . . *postpone* this release."

Students still seemed bewildered as to how they'd gotten out of their seats, but many of them also grumbled that they wouldn't be getting third-party app support that day, after all.

"If only they knew," muttered Stan.

Scarlett gave him a sympathetic smile. "I know what you mean. But it's probably best that they don't."

CHAPTER 26

>>>>>>>>>>>> **A REAL RELIEF TOWN** >>>>>>>>>>>>

Stan felt like he was floating the rest of the school day. He hadn't realized how much it had all been weighing on him. Scarlett had cautioned them not to let down their guard. The Lyre devices might be safe now, but they still had an evil principal who wanted them dead. And that was certainly true.

But now that the Lyre devices weren't scary weapons, Stan could go back to actually enjoying what was honestly some pretty amazing technology. It almost felt like that first day of school, when he'd spent the day being awestruck by how much a well-funded, well-staffed school could accomplish. He even amused himself by switching on the Toon Town filter during math class.

Scarlett remained concerned about hidden surveillance tech in the clubhouse, so they met up briefly after school on the soccer field, where there was definitely no way someone could listen in on their conversations. They also kept their Lyres in the shield bags.

"Wonderful job, everybody," said Scarlett.

"Thanks to an incredible leader," said Stan.

He was surprised to see her smile was a little shy.

"Thanks, Stan. That means a lot to me." Then her smile broadened. "And as our leader, I say we take the rest of the night off. No training, no hacking, no strategizing. Just relaxing."

"I am all for that," said Julien.

"So can we use the Lyre devices however we want now?" asked Stan, shaking his little metallic bag.

"Sort of," said Julien. "Nobody can take control of

them anymore, although Scarlett had me leave it so we can *choose* to switch on the holograms that they want us to see."

"That way we can act natural if we're in a situation where they're expecting us to see something that isn't actually there," interjected Scarlett.

"Right. I set it as a special filter that only the four of us can access called 'Lies,'" said Julien. "Something else to keep in mind: Cobra can still read our messages, see what we're seeing, and listen in on our conversations, because the data goes through their network and it's not end-to-end encrypted. I'll see if I can work out a way to install an encrypted messaging app for the four of us. But right now, if you need to message someone, just be careful what you say."

"And whenever discussing sensitive topics, we should continue to bag them," said Scarlett. "Like I said earlier, we still need to watch our backs with Zartan."

"And the Baroness," said Stan. "I haven't seen her all day, which makes me wonder if she's up to something."

"She's *always* up to something," said Scarlett.

"You two are like bitter rivals or something, huh?" asked Julien.

Scarlett sniffed. "Please, she's got nothing on me."

After the short meeting, Stan and Julien walked home together, recounting their recent adventures with only minimal exaggeration.

"Hey, you want to come over for dinner again?" asked Julien. "I mean, if you can stand more tofu."

"It's better than Cup o' Noodles," said Stan. "But after coming home so late last night, I better message my mom to make sure it's OK."

Stan took his Lyre device out of his pocket and put it on.

STANISŁAW: Mom are you still at work? Julien invited me for dinner again.

LEOKADIA: Yes I will be a few more hours sorry. Make sure you are not a bother for Julien's mother, my little Clash 😶

"I'm good," he told Julien as he pocketed his Lyre again.

When they got to Julien's house, there wasn't any jazz music, but there was a man sitting in the living room. Stan could tell he was tall, even when he was seated, and he had a slightly unkempt Afro and beard that gave him a wacky professor sort of look.

"Dad, you're home already?" asked Julien, looking surprised and pleased.

"Hey, sport. Yeah, your mom and I were just talking about how nice it is for me to be home this early." He turned to a nearby empty chair. "Isn't that right?"

Stan and Julien stared at him. Then at the empty chair.

"Uh, Dad?" said Julien. "Mom's not there."

"Don't be silly. She's right here." He smiled and gestured to the empty chair.

His hands trembling, Julien took out his Lyre and put it on.

"No . . ."

Dread slowly rising in the pit of his stomach, Stan also put on his device and enabled the "Lies" filter. Sure enough, there was a perfect holographic replica of Julien's mom.

"—honestly, how rude!" she was saying. "Hello, boys, I'm right here!"

She waved at them.

"No!" Now Julien actually looked angry.

"What's going on?" asked Stan.

"I just got a message from Michel," his friend said, nostrils flaring. "He has my mom."

CHAPTER 27

>>>>>>>>> **A REAL RESCUE TOWN** >>>>>>>>>

GROUP — Julien March, Stanisław Migda,
Shana O'Hara, 一のゾロ目・嵐影

STANISŁAW: Michel has Julien's mom in the
subbasement!

SHANA: It's a trap

JULIEN: You know I still have to go

一のゾ口目: we will meet you in front of the school. wait for us

"Come on, let's go." Julien tugged Stan's arm as he turned to leave.

"Julien, you're leaving?" his father asked. "But you just got here."

"Take off your Lyre and I'll show you why," Julien said.

His dad chuckled. "What's gotten into you. You're being ridiculous."

"Never mind, then."

Julien left, with Stan hurrying after him.

"Zoro-me's right. We should wait for them before we go in," said Stan.

"We'll see," muttered Julien as they hurried down Main Street.

They reached the school a short time later. The LED sign read:

SPRINGFIELD ACADEMY STUDENTS MAKE THEIR MARK ON THE WORLD!

Stan didn't know where Scarlett was coming from, but he knew the dojo was farther away, so it would take a little longer for Zoro-me to arrive.

"I'm sure we'll only have to wait a few minutes," he said, trying to calm his friend.

"A few minutes?" demanded Julien. "Do you know what that jerk could do to my mom in that time?"

"But he wants *us*, right?" said Stan. "Not her."

"He'll hurt her because he knows it'll hurt me." Julien shook his head. "Nah, I'm going in now. Wait here if you want."

Stan sighed. "You know I can't do that."

The two of them walked up the steps to the front entrance.

"He said it would be unlocked." Julien pushed the door open. "Yep."

"How does that guy have so much power at this school?" Stan asked.

Julien only shook his head, and the two entered the darkened school.

Once inside, they made their way quickly but quietly through the hall. The back of Stan's neck prickled, like he could feel someone watching them. They were blowing past plenty of video cameras, so it was probably inevitable that *somebody* was.

They went down the stairwell that led to the basement, then through the storage area to the door with the keypad security lock. It was also open.

"Such an obvious trap," said Stan.

"Doesn't matter," said Julien. "And he *knows* it."

They walked through the narrow hallway to the elevator, which was open and waiting for them.

Every instinct in Stan's body screamed at him to run. But he couldn't leave Julien to face this alone. And if he had been in his friend's place—if *his* mom had been the one taken—it wouldn't have mattered who had done it. He would have gone after them immediately. So he understood why they couldn't wait.

Even so, he knew they were walking into real trouble.

The elevator let them off at the subway platform. As they walked the length of it to the lab, a train slid into the station and stopped. No one got on or off, and a few seconds later it continued on its way. Stan could see people sitting in the train doing stuff on their Lyre devices, totally unaware of all the awful things going on around them.

It suddenly made him so mad. Even though he'd been genuinely enjoying his Lyre device earlier that day, now he felt like even if these things were "safe," they still got in the way of actually living. Maybe Tommy was right. Maybe people just used them as an escape because they didn't want to admit that their lives were dull and empty.

"We're here," Julien said grimly.

They stared at the wooden door. After a moment, Julien reached for the handle.

"You sure you don't want to wait?" asked Stan.

"It's too late for that."

Stan nodded. "Then let's go."

They opened the door and strode purposefully down the aisle. There was no point in being sneaky. Michel knew they were coming.

At the far end, they saw Michel leaning against one of the doors. He was smiling, but it was a little lopsided because of the large bandage that covered one side of his face.

"Geez, that was actually pretty fast," he said. "Although it looks like you're missing your bodyguards, so that's probably not good. For you."

"Where's my mom?" snapped Julien.

Michel jerked his thumb at the door behind him. "She's in here."

Stan could see her through the window, slumped against the far wall. She had a streak of blood running down from her temple, as though she'd been hit on the head, and she appeared to be unconscious.

"What did you *do* to her?" demanded Julien.

Michel gave an exaggerated shrug. "I could have been more gentle if she'd been wearing a Lyre, but since she wasn't, I had to be a little . . . *direct*."

"You—" Julien took a step forward.

"Whoa!" Michel's eyes sparkled with amusement. "You sure you want to come at me like that when I have your mom hostage?"

Julien gritted his teeth. "What do you want?"

"Actually, I really want *you*." Michel pointed to Stan. "For giving me this beauty mark." He carefully peeled back his bandage and showed them the large burn mark that ran down the side of his face.

Stan winced. "Listen, Michel, that was an accident. I never would have—"

"You think I care?" snapped Michel. "Honestly, I wanted to kidnap *your* mom, but I guess she's too import-ant to DeCobray or something, so I wasn't allowed. But I knew if I took this nerd's mom, he'd come running, and you'd come with him like the self-deluded 'hero' you are."

"I'm not a hero," Stan said.

"*I* know that," said Michel. "Buuuut I'm not sure *you* truly know it yet. Lucky for you, I'm going to give you that lesson. It might be your last, though."

Stan squared his shoulders and got into the stance that Zoro-me had drilled into him for the last week. "Bring it, then."

"What's this? Proper form? Maybe even some balance?" Michel looked impressed. "Have you been *training*?"

"Come find out."

Michel laughed. "Oh, wow, you were totally envision-ing some kind of one-on-one showdown, weren't you. See what I mean? Self-deluded hero."

He tapped something on his Lyre display. The other three doors opened, and a robot emerged from each. They were mostly black and silver, with yellow chest plates showing the red cobra insignia in the center and red glowing eyes on their otherwise featureless faces. In place of a right hand, they each had a long, curved sword blade.

"You like these guys?" Michel looked delighted. "We call them Battle Android Troopers. Or BATs for short. Pretty cool, huh? I've always loved robots. I wasn't allowed to equip them with machine guns or flame throwers, but I guess this is good enough. Especially if it's just you two losers."

Stan knew they were dead. There was no way he could handle Michel *and* three combat robots. Unless . . .

"I don't suppose you could hack into the robots?" he murmured to Julien. "With your Lyre or something?"

He shook his head. "Not in the time it would take them to walk across the room and chop us to pieces."

"Yeah, I figured . . ."

"OK, then!" Michel said brightly. "Time to die!"

Stan had hoped the robots might at least be slow and clunky, but no such luck. They were designed for combat, after all. When Michel tapped his Lyre display, the BATs came at them with alarming speed, their movements almost graceful. They raised their sword blades as they drew near.

"You know what Scarlett would say right now?" Stan asked.

"Yeah . . ." Julien's face screwed up in anguish as he stared through the window at his unconscious mother. "Fine. We run. For now."

They turned and hurried back up the aisle.

But they found two more BATs blocking their path.

Michel barked with laughter. "The look on your faces! I love that you guys don't give up. It makes this all so much more fun."

The two BATs blocking the exit walked toward them, their blades gleaming. There were thick metal shelves on either side, and three BATs still coming up behind them. They were bottled in. There was no escape.

Stan grabbed for stuff on nearby shelves. He found a vial of some kind and chucked it at one of the BATs. The glass shattered against its yellow chest plate and a blue liquid dribbled down, but the BAT didn't even seem to notice. He threw a different one, and this time, the BAT knocked it aside. So not only were they deadly, but they learned. Great.

He glared defiantly at the two BATs and got into his fighting stance, even though he knew it was pointless.

"We're dead," muttered Julien. "I'm sorry for bringing you down here."

"Forget about that," he told his friend. "They won't take us without a fight."

The BATs drew near, lifting their blades as they prepared to strike.

Then a sword tip protruded from the chest of one of the BATs. Sparks flew and the BAT convulsed before falling to the ground with a loud clang.

The person holding the sword was clad in an all-black yoroi with a visor that covered his eyes.

Stan heard a whistling sound. He instinctively ducked as a metal staff swung past and knocked the other BAT's head clean off its shoulders. Sparks flew up from the neck, then the headless body toppled over in a metallic clatter.

There was Scarlett, now dressed in tactical gear and holding the staff in a fighting stance.

"We told you to wait," she said.

Stan turned to the black-clad ninja. *"Zoro-me?"*

"Snake-Eyes," he said.

The two of them moved to stand in front of Stan and Julien, weapons ready as the remaining three BATs approached.

Zoro-me glanced back at Stan, then pointed at Michel. "Clash. Go."

"You want *me* to handle Michel?"

He nodded.

"Snake-Eyes and I will handle the robots," said Scarlett. "You've worked hard, Clash. Show us what you've learned."

"You got this, man," said Julien. "Also, I want a cool code name, too."

Before Stan moved to Springfield, few people had ever expressed confidence in his abilities. He knew his mom loved him, but she just didn't say stuff like that. Only his father . . .

Stan felt the helpless anger rise up in him, but he took a deep breath and channeled that feeling into focus. He had purpose, after all. And he had friends—incredible friends—who believed in him. He wouldn't let them down.

"I'll make you proud, Sensei," he said.

Zoro-me nodded again.

The robots drew near.

Scarlett grinned at Zoro-me. "You ready?"

He shrugged.

She chuckled. "Smart aleck."

Then they charged.

It was incredible to see the two of them really let loose. Scarlett's staff whirled and whistled as she wove between two BATs, lightly blocking their strikes while moving around them to find an opening. Zoro-me wielded his katana like a true warrior, deftly parrying the BATs' strikes, waiting for his moment.

The two managed to maneuver the three BATs to either side of the room, leaving a path down the middle to Michel. He looked like he was about to go after Scarlett, making it three against one.

But Stan blocked his way.

"You are really asking for it, eighth grader," said Michel as he lifted his fists. "Fine, I'll give you the beatdown you want so bad."

Stan took a slow breath, clearing the nerves, and let

go of the fear brought on by their previous fight. Past, future. None of that mattered right now. There was only the present.

Michel came at Stan, and somehow it was now so clear to him. The fake outs, the trickery. That's all Michel was. Intimidation and underhanded tactics, which worked great until you saw them for what they were. The two traded blows back and forth for a few moments, yet neither connected. Then Michel feigned a strike, and Stan could *see* it wasn't real by the way he didn't put any force from his shoulder into it. So he ignored that and went right for the opening it provided, catching Michel in the stomach.

Michel wheezed and stumbled back. "OK, so I guess I have to go all out!"

But that was more intimidation and bluff. It was plain to Stan that Michel's fighting style was no different after that bold declaration. Michel might still be faster and stronger, but Stan realized he could win by being smarter.

They continued to fight, with Michel looking increasingly alarmed. Finally, he started to get desperate and came at Stan with a big roundhouse kick at the side of his head. Had it connected, that would have been it. But

Stan saw it coming, ducked under it, grabbed Michel's leg with both hands, and shoved upward, putting Michel off-balance. Then before he could recover, Stan swept his other leg. Yet even as Michel fell backward, he had tricks. He grabbed for Stan's shirt, intending to pull him down and get him with a grappling hold. But Stan saw that, too, and knocked his hands to either side before he could get a good grip.

So Michel slammed into the ground, and the breath whooshed out of him. While he was momentarily stunned, Stan dropped to one knee and gave him the knockout blow that he had given to Julien's mom. Served him right, hitting somebody's mom like that.

Stan turned quickly to see how Zoro-me and Scarlett were doing. Scarlett had already taken out one BAT by driving her pole through its chest. But the pole had gotten stuck, so she had to abandon it, leaving her weaponless against the remaining, sword-wielding BAT.

Fortunately, Zoro-me had lopped off all four limbs of his BAT, leaving only a twitching robot head and torso on the ground. Scarlett ran at the remaining BAT, then, at the last minute, slid between its legs to where Zoro-me waited. Her back braced against the ground, she lifted both hands, palms up. Zoro-me vaulted off her hands and just as the BAT was turning to face them, he came down with his sword so hard his blade cut diagonally from shoulder to hip, slicing it cleanly in two.

That, decided Stan, was real teamwork.

"Julien!" called Scarlett. "Let's get your mom and get out of here!"

"Shouldn't we, like, call the cops?" asked Stan.

"And how do you plan to do that? With your DeCobray Lyre?" she asked.

He winced. "Forgot about that . . ."

Then she pointed to a camera in the upper corner of the room. "Besides, we just wrecked five of their fancy robots and they know it. They won't risk showing off this kind of tech up on ground level where it might be seen by other people. But if we stay down here, there's no telling what they'll send after us next."

So they helped Julien get his unconscious mom out of the room and escaped.

CHAPTER 28

>>>>>>>>>> **A REAL CLEAN TOWN** >>>>>>>>>>

A few hours later, Anastasia stood in the space that had, until very recently, been Zartan's lab. She checked each room and each shelf to make sure no trace remained. She even knelt down to inspect the corners and make sure no BAT debris had been pushed to one side during the hasty cleanup.

When she found no remaining evidence, she nodded approvingly, then made a video call with her Lyre device.

The Cobra Commander appeared. He wore a blue helmet

with a smooth, featureless mirror mask and was dressed in a blue uniform with a red Cobra insignia on the chest.

"Baroness," the Commander said in his languorous voice.

"Hail Cobra!" said Anastasia.

"Hail Cobra," replied the Commander.

"I have a report, Commander."

"Proceed," said the Commander.

"The lab has been swept clean, and the subway platform has been sealed off so that all trains now bypass the station. If anyone investigates, they will find nothing but a hallway and an empty storage room."

"Well done, Baroness. Stay on the line while I contact Zartan. I want you to hear this as well."

"As you wish, Commander."

A moment later, Zartan's face appeared on her display next to the Commander. He looked uncharacteristically rumpled, his hair mussed, his tie loose. And his expression was at once angry and frightened. This made perfect sense to Anastasia. No doubt he was frustrated at the disastrous results of his latest project, but he also knew that the Cobra Commander did not suffer failure lightly.

His voice was tense as he said, "Hail Cobra!"

"Zartan." The Commander's voice remained as calm as ever. "You've had some trouble of late."

"The Group Aggro test for the Lyre device failed, Commander. I have traced it back to one of my students, who apparently was able to infiltrate our servers and—"

"Yes, I know," said the Commander.

Zartan looked stunned. "You . . . know?"

"Indeed, I knew before your test even took place, and I let it happen."

"But . . ." Zartan looked utterly mystified. *"Why?"*

"The Lyre was always something of a niche project. Most of our customers prefer more . . . *direct* methods. I indulged you for a time because I saw some tangential value, but I think we've gotten about as much as we're going to get out of it. Besides, I was curious to see what those plucky little upstarts were capable of. One should never dismiss promising young talent out of hand. If we did that, we would never have gained such a model Cobra as the darling Baroness here."

"You honor me, Commander," Anastasia said promptly, a rush of pride running through her.

"But, Zartan, there *is* something that troubles me . . ." Now the Commander's voice took on a harder tone. "While you were fussing about with your little therapy project, you somehow allowed the Arashikage ninja clan to infiltrate your school."

Zartan blanched. "The Arashikage clan?"

"Yes," said the Commander.

Now fear was the dominant emotion on Zartan's face. "C-Commander, I assure you—"

"Enough." The Commander cut him off. "We will discuss the consequences of your negligence upon your return."

"My return?"

"You are recalled to base immediately."

Zartan did his best to hide his dread and despair but was not entirely successful. This pleased Anastasia greatly. She'd never liked Zartan. Too full of himself, and much too vain.

"Yes, Commander," he said weakly.

"Hail Cobra," said the Commander by way of dismissal.

"Hail Cobra," Zartan said, looking like he might actually throw up. Then his connection ended.

"Now, Baroness."

"Yes, Commander!" Anastasia said eagerly.

"I will be sending along a replacement principal soon enough who has some . . . *interesting* ideas. I will also confer with some experts on how best to handle our ninja infestation. In the meantime, I would like you to keep an eye on these *Average Joes*, as they insist on calling themselves, but take no direct action. For now."

"As you wish, Commander!"

"Hail Cobra."

"Hail Cobra!"

Once the connection ended, Anastasia allowed herself a happy sigh. She had been right to steer clear of Michel's reckless revenge scheme. Now she was the only one left at the school that the Commander could truly rely on. Her patience and diligence were finally paying off.

This was only the beginning for her.

A REAL NORMAL TOWN

Stan and his friends had taken Ms. March directly to the hospital. They knew it might be infested with Cobra agents, but what else could they do? Even so, Stan was not particularly surprised when Julien told him the next day that his mom didn't remember anything. She said she'd been at home, playing her piano, and the next thing she knew, she was in the hospital.

Hauser did the school announcements the next morning, saying that Principal Zartan had to leave suddenly due to a family emergency and did not expect to return. Hauser would serve as acting principal until the school board chose a new one.

It was surreal how normal the school day seemed. Everyone went about their day, blissfully unaware that they were being used as lab rats for an evil organization that made everything from mood-controlling headsets to killer robots. Fortunately, the Average Joes club was there to keep an eye on things.

Anastasia greeted Stan warmly when they crossed paths and asked him how he was settling into Springfield. No more veiled threats, no more pressure. She acted like she was merely a concerned upperclassman. He played along. Better to keep his enemies close, he decided. He was sure she was up to something, but there wasn't much he could do about it yet.

Dr. Hauser was not pleased with Stan and his friends, of course. He called the Joes into his office, and after he'd turned on his Wi-Fi scrambler, he gave them an earful.

"I *told* you not to endanger yourselves, and yet here we are. You do realize that all four of you nearly got yourselves killed last night?"

"With respect," said Scarlett, "we also saved Julien's mom's life."

"But don't you see how this escalates?" demanded Hauser. "You broke into their labs and injured Michel, then he retaliates with greater force, putting Ms. March in jeopardy in the process. Then you respond by trashing millions of dollars in Cobra tech. Do you think they won't come back with something worse?"

"What should we have done instead?" she asked plaintively.

He opened his mouth to say something, then stopped. He tried again, but stopped himself again. Finally he rubbed his temples and said, "From now on, just talk to me *before* you do anything reckless like that. Understood?"

"Of course," said Scarlett.

Stan and Julien exchanged a look. They knew what *that* meant.

CHAPTER 30

It was a typical evening at the O'Hara house:

"Where have *you* been? Drinking at the bar again?!"

"Bah, I don't want to hear it from you!"

"Too bad! Here I am making dinner and keeping this family together, while you—"

"Your dinners are lousy, and so is this family! You're all a bunch of lazy ingrates!"

"Both of you stop yelling! I can't hear my video!"

Scarlett sighed and focused on the ravioli on her plate

as her father, mother, and younger brother all shouted around her. Her father, a thickset man with the same red hair as Scarlett, had come home reeking of sour beer again. Her mother had immediately started cursing him out, even as she slapped spoonfuls of heated ravioli from the can onto plates for Scarlett and her brother, Paul. Paul barely noticed any of it, so long as he could continue to watch videos on the tablet he'd received from Springfield Elementary. A DeCobray brand tablet, of course.

This was all so routine for Scarlett that it was easy to block out by now. She did keep an eye on her father, however. In case he tried to hit her mother again. Scarlett had stopped him the last time. He hadn't tried again since, but she wasn't about to let her guard down.

Once she'd eaten enough ravioli, she asked, "May I be excused?"

"Sure, hun," said her mother.

She took her plate over to the sink and began to wash it.

"And you, girl!" her father shouted at her back. "You think you're so much better than us?"

"I'm no better," she said quietly as she dried her dish and put it away.

"You're darn right!" her father yelled. "You're nothing but an ungrateful leech!"

"Don't you talk to my daughter like that!" yelled her mother.

"She's my daughter, too, and I'll talk to her however I like!"

Scarlett went to her room and closed the door behind her to muffle at least some of their noise. As she walked over to her desk, she brushed her fingertips across her beloved chess set. It had been a gift from Yawarakai-sensei. Each piece was hand-carved and made to look like something from feudal Japan, from the pagoda rooks and samurai knights to the emperor kings.

She sat down at her desk and booted up her cobbled together PC. Scarlett knew that smartphones were a privacy black hole, but a custom-built computer loaded with a self-compiled, open-source Linux operating system was as secure as you chose to make it. The only real issue was using the free DeCobray citywide Wi-Fi without letting it sniff her traffic. But that was what SSH, proxies, and VPN tunnels were for. She wasn't nearly as tech-savvy as Julien, but she knew her way around a command line.

First she opened the encrypted IRC channel she shared with Zoro-me.

RED: parents at it again

SNAKE: i can still ask my uncles if they will let you move in

RED: i know, thanks :) but it's not that bad

SNAKE: you are just acclimated to how bad it is

RED: maybe so. i promise i'll tell you if it gets too much for me

SNAKE: thank you

Next she checked her email client. She generally used

onetime disposable addresses for most communication, so she rarely received messages. But there was something she had been hoping to see.

And it was finally there.

It had no sender name and no subject. It was a disposable email address similar to the kind she used. Just a pseudo-random hash of letters and numbers.

But she knew instantly that it was them.

She opened the plain text message, complete with single-use encryption key attached. It said:

```
You and your team are doing excellent
work. Disregard Duke's orders. He's been
in that position far too long and has
become complacent. He's unwilling to
accept just how dire the situation has
become. Cobra is planning something big,
and bold action is what's needed now,
before it's too late.


Await further instructions. And welcome to
the Anti-Venom Coalition.
```

Scarlett grinned. Finally, all her patience and diligence were paying off.

RED: at last, direct contact from AVC

SNAKE: what's next?

RED: waiting to find out. but I'll tell you one thing—this is only the beginning for us.

ACKNOWLEDGMENTS

I owe a great deal to Larry Hama. When he was working at Marvel back in the early 1980s, he was given a bunch of character designs and told to write a comic based on them. Many creators have contributed wonderful things to the franchise since, but a G.I. Joe without Snake-Eyes or the villainous Cobra? I think it's safe to say that this book would not have been possible without Larry Hama.

But it's not merely this book that I owe to Larry Hama. Being a tad unconventional, it was difficult and often frightening for me growing up in the early '80s in Ohio. G.I. Joe offered a safe haven. The boys in my class loved the lasers and tanks, while I loved the cool ladies and flamboyant villains. And of course, everyone loves ninjas. So the net result was that I could express my whole-hearted passion for something and not get picked on for it! We are talking years in which I basically got a free pass from daily cruelty because I was the G.I. Joe expert, and that was considered pretty cool back then. Thanks for that, Mr. Hama!

Now when I go back and look at those early comics, I see an astonishingly progressive view for that era. The chief medical examiner was a Black man? The head of counterintelligence was a woman? This was mind-blowing stuff back in the '80s, and Hama just dropped it in there, like that's how it was supposed to be—and he was correct. He also drew upon his personal experiences as a Vietnam veteran and Japanese American to introduce a whole host of ideas I would likely never have come across otherwise. Larry Hama taught me that anyone from anywhere could become a real American hero.

And of course, I am also grateful to the many people who worked on this book with me. Thanks to my acquiring editor, Russ Busse, for believing in this project in the first place, and my current editor, Anne Heltzel, for stepping into the thick of it with bold enthusiasm. Thanks also to the legendary Phil Noto for the wonderful cover and the good folks at Hasbro for giving me the keys to this particular kingdom. And as always, thank you to my agent, Jill Grinberg, and the very real American heroes at JGLM.